Go, Cockaroo

The first novel by

Cody Spotanski

This book is a work of fiction. Any references to historical events, real people, or real places are used fictitiously. Other names, characters, places, and events are products of the author's imagination, and any resemblance to actual events or places or persons, living or dead, is entirely coincidental.

Copyright © 2019 by Cody Spotanski

All rights reserved, including the right to reproduce this book or portions thereof in any form whatsoever.

Edited by Lexi Harris

Cover Illustration by Allison Plume — Instagram @allisonplume

Portions of this work first appeared in *The Oddville Press*.

Without the support of Randy Leifeste, Jennifer Hollingshead, Susan Beaubien, Marc Leifeste and all of the gracious folks that frequent The Castell General Store, the adventure in these pages would not have been possible.

> *"Ya gotta want it..."*
> — **Randy Leifeste**

CHAPTER 1 ...
A Sage in Sweats

I pulled off the highway, onto a side road and into the parking lot of an army surplus store somewhere in the middle of Kansas to stretch my legs and browse the broken shelves. My savings were growing thin, so I'd left my wallet in the van. An impulse buy, when you're traveling cross-country on a nothing budget, is derelict and irresponsible and not very minimalistic. But, I'd never seen a military-grade hammock tent. Sixty-two dollars. I went back out to get my wallet. In school, we watched a war documentary and it made me feel eager for an hour and a half but never in a way that made me want to join a war. Those boys did a lot of sleeping in those pea-green cocoons suspended over Vietnam. I was attracted to the camping and the cigarettes and the small ways the soldiers had of distinguishing their uniforms from one another and making them look relaxed and their own. I think I was more into the nostalgia and style of it all than anything ugly like fighting or commitment. Imperfect young men like me just want to be soldiers, and most soldiers just want to be home.

I put the folded hammock under one of the benches in the rear of the van and got back on the road. Around 2 p.m., I pulled up my map. Cane licked my face. Wichita was a few hours away and I didn't want to drive all night again, half-lost, half-hallucinating.

We made it downtown that afternoon and found a YMCA. I showered in my sandals, dried off, saw three bare asses, one penis, five nipples and a Band-Aid in the locker room. I dressed and walked out past a row of treadmills. There must have been thirty of them. Everybody was sweating. You see all these bouncing heads and shoulders in a perfect line. A limp in a row of treadmills is easy to spot, so is a fart. When you fart on a treadmill there's no wind to carry it away. All you can do is stir it up with your legs and hope everyone else is breathing through their mouths. In the hallway, there was a window that overlooked the indoor swimming pool. I've always thought about fixing a mixed drink and lounging in a layback chair down by the edge of the water and whistling at the retired school teachers who swim laps just to move their bones and get away from their husbands for the night. I walked out the front door and into a city at dusk, looking for a drink.

    I found a spot. It was toward the center of the city, west of the YMCA. I always tried to find the historic districts. There, the architecture keeps me believing in things and the girls are more my type. I hadn't talked to anyone that day besides Cane and the attendant at the surplus store. Neither of them had much to say. So, when I ordered my drink, my words came out too loud like too much was riding on them. I wanted them to pulsate and have consequence but they didn't. The words I used must have worked well enough though, because a minute or two later, I had a beer in front of me. I sat there wishing the bartender might have wanted to hear me talk more.

    I was sitting next to a short unathletic man in his thirties. He was a jumpy little guy with simple features and short dark hair combed against his head like it was wet. He was draped in cheap sweats. He was a modern slob, the type who doesn't care about dressing for effect – they pull on elastic pants every morning because it's what their mothers filled their drawers with, and it's easier not to challenge themselves. He had a small book on the bar opened to about the middle. Next to the paperback was his notebook. He was writing in it hard and heavy like he was trying to carve them into the bar top. His head was tilted over his half-drunk beer, and in the low light of the barroom, the oily skin on his forehead looked pale and dense. I sat there switching back and forth between staring at the wall and staring into the top of my black beer. The snow was blowing up against the window behind us. I worried about Cane curled up in his sleeping bag in the passenger seat of the van. I left him a bowl of water and we had split a burger for lunch. I still worried thinking about what some lady said to me at a Wyoming laundromat, claiming I don't know how to take care of a dog, and that I'm treating him bad, and that I'm going to end up killing him leaving him in a car like that, and that she's just worried about the dog and don't care one way or the other about myself or what I wanted to do to my own life, just wanted the best for the dog and was just looking out for the dog.

    I had enough of the wall and enough of a third beer to climb out of the silence I'd built around myself. The bar was crackling with townies, freaks and hipsters, but the itchy guy with the book, beer and notebook looked harmless. Like the type I could manage. I asked him about his writing. I could tell, based on his concentration and zeal, that he'd come at me in one of two ways. Either he would ignore me like I was just another muted TV on the wall, trying to distract him from his work, or, he would recognize my curiosity and cling to it like he was clinging to the pages in front of him. He clung, and I immediately considered turning slowly away from him and resuming my engagement with the wall. But, I'm a friendly Midwestern kid so I listened and nodded.

    He was transcribing a lengthy piece of text, a bent-up copy of a book written by an old philosopher that, if you consider yourself a sensitive worldly kind of person, like I sometimes do, you think you should have read, or be aware of, or at least tell people you were aware of or have read. He was copying it word-for-word. He tried describing some of the book's arguments to me, but couldn't. While he struggled to explain another man's ideas, he gestured like a nervous maestro

7

in sweats with his small hairy knuckles dancing like spiders in the air between our barstools. The man said he copied the book four times, and when I asked him why, he paused at the question. The guy fucking paused...a lot. He was sort of hard to talk to. He had these big animated pauses full of hand waves and gasps. Stops and starts. He'd close his eyes and twist his hand around like he was trying to waft an answer out of the air into his head. When the wafting didn't work, he'd make a fist on the bar top and drop his chin onto it like a football on a tee. I thought, at first, he paused so long because his mind was vast and it took him a minute to mine its gooey lattice and find an answer to the question. Eventually, though, after a few long minutes of watching him struggle, and silently rooting for him to find the words, I realized that instead, his mind was flat from hours of thoughtlessly transcribing someone else's work. Flat like a tile floor that someone threw a bucket of mop water across. Wet but held nothing.

From what I understood of his frustrated mumbling, I ascertained that this Greek philosopher, this lecturer, who was born a slave, had developed a manual on living. Tips and tricks to use throughout your day to cultivate a wise demeanor.

1. Sacrifices are to be made.
2. Do not stress that which is out of your control.
3. Dress plainly.
4. Avoid casual sex.

I was a layman carpenter and a junior college dropout, but I peddled in bullshit and could maneuver my way through an inflated philosophical conversation. So, I responded when thoughts came into my head. My participation seemed to excite him. He was a lonely dude, and not by choice.

I told him that maybe, like an actor, he was vigorously trying to memorize the script to an ideal consciousness. He was a tennis-shoe monk wannabe trying to blur the line between himself and the text.

"You want to live the book, man," I said. "That's why you're so into it. Trying to beat it into your head. That's the only way to really absorb this stuff. Advice only works if you practice it. Self-help never worked on me. It only makes me more anxious."

He liked that. His gaze receded from my face and his eyes moved around the room escorted by a smirk. I finished the last warm sip of my beer and set the glass on the wooden bar.

The temperature outside was dropping and I could feel the crowd lighten. The man ripped out a page from his notebook and scribbled down, The Art of Living/Epictetus, then handed it to me. The name of the book joined a long list of names of books I've considered reading but haven't because the changing colors of my phone are too soothing, and a blank wall doesn't ask anything of me. I thanked him and left the small tavern. I made the walk through the dead city back to my castle: a yellow 2005 Dodge Sprinter Van in a parking lot of a YMCA.

The snow hushed the streets, and the few blocks I had to cross were industrial and sleeping. The wind had the resolve to cut through my coat, but the beer had me alive and moving. My hands were buried in my pockets and my armpits were tight and sweaty and shivering. My boots on the wet sidewalk kicked a lonesome sound complemented by the occasional humorless car scraping by. I liked walking in those boots because they were heavy and it felt like I was getting something done when I covered ground in them, like a task was being handled.

When I reached the van, I was too drunk to drive around an unfamiliar city and look for a place more abandoned. Plus, I always figured the Young Men's Christian Association was Christian enough to let me sleep in their parking. Not that I slept. Either way, I never stayed for more than a night. I pulled around to an unlit corner for the sake of discretion.

I put the Dodge in park and shook in the driver's seat while I patted Cane on the head. The van meant warmth and rest, but rest usually meant another chore. I walked to the back and sat on the bench. In front of me on the table, in a small tin tray, an old smelly cigarette butt sat cold. I picked it up and lit it. I stood and opened the overhead air vent and flipped the switch to the fan but it didn't come on.

"Fuck," I said. I flipped the switch back and forth a couple of times. That never works, but we do it anyway. I knew what the problem was, and I knew what I had to do. I sat back down and sucked at my cigarette until it burned my finger. Then, I got up and lifted the seat of the bench. It hinged open and inside the compartment were my tools. I grabbed a dirty white rag that was bunched up in the corner of the box. I aimed the flashlight on my phone into the compartment and picked through the noisy silver wrenches. After I found the right size, I shut the lid, opened the sliding door to the van and walked around to the rear of the vehicle. I lied down and the snow caressed my back. My phone rested next to my shoulder, shining its light up into the belly of the van. The bolt holding the cable from the battery isolator was corroded, and the connection between it and the ring terminal was poor. My auxiliary battery had gone dead and the isolator wasn't charging it when I drove. I flipped the switch to shut the power off from the isolator. I unscrewed the nut from the bolt and cleaned them both with the rag. The tail of the cloth hung in my face and smelled like motor oil. I replaced the nut and flipped the power back on.

Inside the van, I slammed the sliding door as hard as I could but I knew it wouldn't make a difference. The thing would never shut all the way. Something was bent inside the mechanics of the latch and it kept the door propped open an inch maybe an inch and a half. It's hell when you're driving, too. Wind shoves itself in and you can't hear anything but your thoughts. In hot weather, bugs sneak in at night.

Inside the cab, my hands were cold and painful. They bumbled and didn't follow directions well, but somehow, they lit the stove, or maybe they didn't. Maybe I just stared at it long enough until the burner sparked a fire. I held my hands in the flame until I heard my skin sizzle. I spit the taste of cigarette into the stainless-steel sink. It slid and bubbled over dried black specks in the drain.

    The bench, which housed my tools, was U-shaped and when I lowered the table into the gap between the benches, it made a flat surface, my bed. I took my boots off. The solitude settled into my mind as I lied across the thin cushions. I tucked my face against the cool nylon fabric of my sleeping bag.

    Sometimes beer will get me an hour or two, but not that night in Kansas. I don't know what I was expecting. I guess I'd hoped the conversation with the mum philosopher would wear me out, but it only seemed to stimulate me more. I lied there and got no relief. The wind shook the van a little. The hours crawled by. At times, I thought I'd die from loneliness, the kind of loneliness you feel when you realize there's no one within a hundred miles that knows your name. It's the opposite of claustrophobia, but just as suffocating, and it comes at you in thumps. Every time I closed my eyes, I was in St. Louis again; in the courtroom, in the hospital, in my sister's kitchen not eating. I should have known not to drive through the Midwest. The insomnia was worse the closer I got to Missouri. The guilt waited at the state line with its arms crossed. It's a pang of lyrical guilt whose song I hummed with the same stone in my throat, the same sweat on my neck.

    I'm not sure how long I'd been staring at the ceiling shivering before I noticed the headache. Cane was moaning and whimpering from the back of his throat, the way a dog will do. I tore my eyes from the ceiling. The flame on the stove had been blown out by the penetrating wind, but the gas was still whistling. The dog was facing the door, and when I moved, he looked over at me, then back at the door and shifted his front paws in anticipation like they were standing on something hot.

    "It's too cold," I said. "Piss on the floor."

    The only reason I wasn't farther south that late in the season was that I got offered a job painting a pinball hall in

White Fish, Montana, and the guy ended up liking my work and I ended up liking the fishing. So, when he told me he owned a bowling alley and a tobacco shop too, I stayed for another month to do some plumbing and carpentry work for him. Before that, it was New England, and Florida and Georgia and who knows where else. One night, a year or so in, I sat at the table in the van with a gas station map of the United States and traced the route I'd taken since leaving home. I stared at the lines scratched across the map and felt shame bouncing around the country like a fly looking for a hole in a jar. Cane whined again a little louder and a little more intentional.

"Alright. We're going to Texas."

I unzipped my sleeping bag from the inside and stepped sockless into my cold boots and wobbled dizzily, the propane still expanding through the lines. When I reached for the knob on the stove, the gas stopped. I stood there with my hand extended. I opened the cabinet below the sink, reached down and shook the propane tank. Empty. I started breaking down the camper and the headache wouldn't quit. I reached for my jacket and stumbled. I thought maybe if I was lucky, the gas would knock me out and I could sleep for the first time in days. I put away a few loose dishes and brushed some cigarette ash off the counter. It fell onto Cane's black back. He looked up at me.

"Give me a minute," I said. "Where's my phone?" I looked all over the floor and under the sleeping bag. I opened the sliding door and snow blew in. It had snowed another inch while I was lying in my bed busted and shaking. I looked around on the ground and the phone was under the van, still lit. I was reaching for it when I heard shouting carried by the wind from the other side of the parking lot. I stood up curiously, my head filled with blood. I walked in my long underwear and jacket out into the darkness. There were men out there — a whole company of soldiers in the middle of a Great Plains parking lot blizzard. I shuffled in my untied boots, and as I got closer, gunfire lit up the night. Mortar shells whistled overhead. Three men in green t-shirts and battle fatigues ran past without noticing me. They held their helmets on top of their heads, then slid on their stomachs against the curb, coiling behind it for cover. Their faces looked deliberate. They shot blindly over the curb into an alley across the street. A string of bullets ran up the side of the YMCA building and hit the illuminated sign, knocking out the big red "C." All around me, soldiers were breaking down tents, screaming and firing into the black corners of the city. A mortar hit the streetlight in the middle of the parking lot and kicked it from the asphalt. I shook my head.

"They followed us," I said, and looked down at Cane. He was pissing on my boot. "No!" I yelled. I started hopping around in the snow, shaking my foot out to the side trying to dry it when a GI ran up to me, grabbed me by the arm and pulled me down into a crouching position. He held his rifle up over his head, protecting himself from shrapnel. He had a blonde mustache and his hand was warm and wet with blood.

"Jesus Christ!" the man said. "Get dressed, Porter! There's gooks all over this ridge." With his rifle in his hand, he pointed his finger up at an abandoned bread factory two blocks east. "We're being picked up across the valley. The birds can't land here."

A hand-rolled cigarette struggled to stay lit in his mouth against the wind and snow. "And get that goddamned dog on a leash before you get it killed." He looked at me long and serious. Snowflakes beat against his forehead and melted and rolled like sweat down around his pinched eyebrows. A token was tucked into the band of his tattered green helmet. It was a poker chip. Red and white, with a picture of a snarling bull in the center. Four soldiers with green packs slung over their shoulder ran behind him, slipping in the snow. He turned to his left, put the rifle against his shoulder and fired five shots into a building across the street.

"She said I could come back whenever I want," I told him. He didn't seem to hear me. He looked over his shoulder and the cigarette burned red around the edge. I spoke louder this time. "I'm going to see Marla in the spring. Maybe summer."

He looked back at me and yelled. "Feed that goddamned dog something!" Then he ran away into the darkness with his head low and his rifle in one hand down below his hip.

I closed my eyes hard and pressed my hand against my forehead. When I opened them, there was nothing but an expanse of unbroken snow. There was no bloody handprint on my shoulder, nothing was left but a headache. The city block was silent again except for a car alarm ringing in the distance. As I walked back to the camper, the buildings that stood around the parking lot began to lean inward on top of me like cold drunken giants trying to bum a ride to Texas. I did my best to ignore them.

I was a few steps away from the van when my boot went through the snow and asphalt like a ghost passing through a wall. I fell forward and told my hands to brace for the ground but they stayed at my side. By the time my face hit, I was unconscious.

There's no way to know how long I was out, but, when I woke up, it was still dark and the blood that came from my nose, and the blood that came from my forehead, had coalesced and frozen into a cast around my head and fixed it to the asphalt.

CHAPTER 2 ...
Dripping Dreams

When I passed through Oklahoma City, the sun had turned the cold eastern horizon pink. Somewhere past Dallas I pulled off in a patch of grass at the end of a rural airstrip and played fetch with the dog. Small private jets and prop planes took off and landed on the other side of the chain-link fence. I pulled out my phone and scrolled through to find Hardy's number. A graduate research assistant from Alpine, Texas, I met him when I was painting a ranch home in New Mexico the year prior. He was on location, studying the mule deer population at the time. We hiked around the property together, pointed at lizards and fished. Like most of the friends I made on the road, I imagined I'd never see him again, though he told me to call if I ever found myself in Texas. I was surprised he picked up.

"Hey, man. What's happening?" I said, trying to sound enthused and fully awake.

"Sorry, sir, dropped my old phone off a crag. Lost everybody. Who's this?"

"It's Luke. From Missouri. We went fishing together on George's ranch."

"Gosh dang, Luke! Where you at these days? Looking for work?"

"Yeah, I'm in Texas. I'm always looking for work, unless I'm not." I tried to laugh. "And a pretty place to park if I can find it."

"Gosh, it's good hearing from yuh, bub. If you're gonna be around Texas awhile, I got some people that might be able to put you up. It's a resort type place ran by a couple old hippies out of Glen Rose. I'm in with them real close. I'm headed over in a few days. Running a study out there."

"They got a warm bed?"

"Oh, shoot yeah," Hardy said. "I'll see if I can get you set up. Should be no problem," he said. "But, I guess I should tell you now, the ladies…"

A prop plane sputtered overhead, teetering in liftoff. My head rang and I disappeared in the noise. The world went calm for me for a second. Cane stared at the slobbery ball in my hand. I couldn't hear a thing Hardy said.

"Alright, buddy," I said. "Send me the address."

"Ok, partner, just tap the call button when you get to the gate."

"I'll figure it out. See you in a couple days."

The drive through the purlieu of Dallas started ugly like it does when leaving all cities, but, eventually, I found myself being raised and dropped on the backroads of central Texas. Penetrating the wide-open secrets of this country had the dog and me drooling out the windows of my truck, my scabs colliding with the late winter air. I had a few days to kill, so I kept my eye out for a campground. I found one outside of Erath County. It was rocky, and private and empty like I wanted it to be. At the entrance was a drop box. Above it was a hand-painted sign that said, "WELCOME TO ERATH – LOOKS LIKE EARTH, BUT A LITTLE JUMBLED UP." It was five-dollars a night. I dropped a ten into the box and lied in the camper with the door as open as my head. The late February sun pressed itself onto the roof of the van and tried to warm it. A potter wasp bumped its way through the door and smelled around for a place to build her nest. I watched her from my bed as she worked. My dad had explained to me once how wasps mix their saliva with mud and use it to build a home. For two days, the wasp and I carried out our daily chores like silent roommates; me doing my dishes in the hose water, her carrying paste in her mouth, sticking it to the ceiling then leaving to get more mud.

After two nights in Erath, I peeled the beginnings of the clay nest off the ceiling with a spatula and broke down camp. I drove for about an hour and finally made it to the address Hardy had given me. I pulled off the farm-to-market road and up to a high black gate that locked across a red gravel path. The fence was thick and ornamented with metalwork. Welded to the spindles were black cast-iron silhouettes of African oryx, cheetahs, giraffes, and some other herding animals that I couldn't identify. *Dripping Dreams Ranch*, it said above the entrance. A grey keypad dangled from a small post in the driveway. I drove up to it, reached through the window, and tapped the call button, staring wide-eyed down the black lens of a security camera. The line rang all the way through and clicked. I tried twice more and got nothing. I pulled out my phone to call Hardy but didn't have service. It was a cold grey day. I'd been driving all morning on two coffees and no breakfast, and needed to pee ten miles ago. By the time I'd reached the gate, it was a pressing issue. Exiting the van, I walked around behind the intercom and pissed. Where was everybody? Just then, a voice exploded from the speaker.

"Come here, yuh little fucker," a breathless old woman yelled, then I heard running feet and a wailing sound. I waited frozen, still peeing behind the camera.

"Hello," said a second voice, this one, another woman, was speaking closer to the receiver. "Hello?" she said. "Is anyone there? I don't see anyone in the driver's seat. I don't see anyone in the driver's seat, Cookie," she said.

"Call the Sheriff. They left a car bomb at the gate!" Cookie yelled from the far side of what sounded like a large echoing room.

"Oh! No! Hello!" I said, shuffling backward around the post to the front of the speaker, leaving a shaky trail of steaming piss in the dirt. "I'm Luke Porter," I said, bending close to the camera.

"Oh, you must be Hardy's friend," she said, collecting herself, "Hujambo, Luke. I'm Sarah." She sounded like an actress, and her words poured through the intercom settleing like a puddle of caramel on the red dirt road.

"Yes, ma'am," I said.

"Why'd you leave your car, dude?"

"I called three times and couldn't get an answer, so I was walking around looking for another entrance," I said, zipping my pants.

"Oh no, we only have the one. I apologize for the delayed response. If you *did* ring all those times, my assistant and I mustn't have heard it. We have goats."

"Ah," I said.

"Are you some kind of fighter, Luke?"

"Excuse me, ma'am?"

"Your face," she said.

"It's freezing out here, ma'am. You mind if I come inside? Hardy is expecting me."

"Yes, totally cold," Sarah said. "I'm sorry. Come in. Cookie and I will be busy with the goats this afternoon, but we'll meet you all for dinner tonight. Welcome to Dripping Dreams." A giraffe cracked down the middle, and the two halves of the gate drew back from one another. I got in the driver's seat and drove through. I crept a half-mile down the rutted dirt road with the back doors of the van rattling. When I came upon a ranch house, I saw Hardy carrying totes of gear from his truck to the front door. The house was single-storied, burgundy and pristine. He saw me coming, dropped the boxes and started waving with a big wide swing of his arm. His elbow bent embarrassingly over the top of his head. He was tall and bobbed when he walked. He had a long oval face, a long oval nose and one long oval front tooth. Straight dirt-brown clumps of hair hung at the same length across his forehead. A nerd in rancher's clothing.

"Hey, bub!" he said when I stepped out of the car.

"What's going on, man? Good to see you." We hugged.

The compression puffed the smell of my unwashed body up through the neck of my coat and into my face.

"What you been up to?" he asked. "I bet a lot, huh? You been fishing?" His words were loopy but sober sounding.

"A little. Gonna try to land a Guadalupe Bass while I'm in Texas. Been hearing about 'em," I said.

"Oh, they're around. I know a place above Austin's got 'em on the Colorado. Boy, you look like you need some rest," he said. "Golly! There he is!" Cane ran up and greeted Hardy at his knees. The tall young man bent down and petted the good dog behind both ears. "He's gonna love it here. We'll have to tie him up when we go out, though.

"Yeah, I figured. He's a scientist, too," I told Hardy. "Always sniffing. Always curious." He stood up from the dog and turned to face the house with his hands in his coat pockets.

"This is where we're staying, Uwanja. It's the smallest house. The hunters will be in Casa Simba when they get here, so we'll have this one to ourselves," he said, walking up to the porch. I followed him in. The main room of the house was open and full of wood. Wood trim, wood tables, sanded and shellacked wood walls. Real cedar. Probably local and expensive. It was done better than I've seen elsewhere in the Southwest. Shona figurines of lovers embracing decorated darkly stained wooden tables. African masks and walking sticks sat in the corners. Carved wooden elephants and gazelles walked across the mantle above the sandstone fireplace. So much wood, you could smell it.

"Who's Uwanja?" I asked.

"No, it ain't no one. It's Swahili. It means 'field,'" he said.

"Field, huh?"

"Yes, sir. Ever think you'd learn African in Texas? Sarah spent a month over there when she was getting sober. I think it really took." He bit his bottom lip with his oval tooth and nodded contently while his eyes scanned the room. "Hey, bub, I'm hungry," he said and swatted my chest with the back of his hand. He turned and bobbed through to the kitchen. Walking away, he hooked his long finger into his gums and pulled out a plug of black tobacco. It dripped syrupy from his fingertips onto the bright cedar floor as he passed through the doorway.

    I slid into a couch in front of a large window and crossed my legs. On a heavy wooden coffee table in front of me, sat a thin photo book. It was white and waxy and professionally bound. I picked it up and opened it to the middle. The pictures in the book were taken to showcase the ranch and all of its heartwarming points of interest. Some tripping hippie Texan in cargo shorts with a camera must have put it together as a favor, or possibly as payment for a weekend stay. The quality of the photos suggested that he was probably a hobbyist or maybe a local newspaper guy. I flipped back to the cover page. There was a little blurb centered on it typed in a big curly kind of font. It read:

Dripping Dreams

She is a gathering place for rejuvenation, nonindulgence and self-reflection. The keepers of this space are committed to using restorative land practices, organic farming and natural resource conservation —eperience serenity, sobriety and wholeness during your stay. Guests can embark on spiritual quests, study group yoga, encounter the exotic, and find themselves, lost, in one of three stone labyrinths.

    I flipped through the pictures looking for Uwanja. Wild gourd, Texas prickly poppy, coyotes and prairie dogs were all there. The big glossy pages rolled and popped under my fingertips. I eventually found a photo of the house. Petite and bright and well lit, but poorly framed, there was Uwanja. I moved the book closer to my face, looking for myself on the couch in the window. But the curtains were closed, so I stood up and opened them. I looked back at the book. Nothing changed.

Hardy came out of the kitchen, realizing he hadn't asked me if I wanted anything to eat.

"Bet you're hungry," he said.

"Yeah."

For lunch, we at whitetail deer burgers with mustard on white bread. He told me how he shot the doe with his bow the week before last.

"She came trotting up to the feeder right at dusk. I could hardly see my pins, but I let it fly and caught her in the spine. I haven't missed in seven years," Hardy said. I asked him how he killed the mustard. He poked the sizzling burger on the skillet with his fork. "At dinner, you'll meet Sarah and Cookie, and afterward, you can help us collect some data."

I didn't want to sit around after lunch, so I went outside and strolled around the cottage while Hardy unpacked. The Uwanja house was on one of the highest points on the property. I walked across a high-grass pasture full of ash junipers.

At the edge of the pasture, I noticed a large wooden observation deck that hung over a cliff. I wandered with my hands in my pockets out toward the center of the deck and tripped on a copper plate in the floor. Bolted to one of the floorboards, the square plate read: "Star Pad" in oxidized letters. I looked up at the sun and squinted. A banister enclosed the deck and on the side that hung out over the precipice, a large brass bell swung in place of the railing. A thick mesquite limb was sitting against the spindles. I walked over to the bell and saw another plate built into the floor below it. On the copper plaque, there was a poem written in the same raised weathered lettering:

Ricochet

The bell over Chalk Mountain
rings out across the confluence

and bounces back
into itself and into the one who struck it,
sharing its gift.

The star sped ringing,
from the tolling bell, ricochets
through the shell
where my substance used to stand.
All that is left now
is awe, a desire to return,
and Dripping Dreams.

There was white bird shit splattered across the word "sharing." I flicked the bell with the back of my finger.

That night, Hardy took me to the main house and gave me a tour before dinner.

"This is the lion house," he said, "Casa Simba. It's fit for *pamperin'*," he said. He curled the corner of his mouth like he was biting the inside of his cheek. "It's done up even nicer and woodier than Uwanja," he said. It was also a ranch-style house, but four-times the size of our cabin. He showed me the whole thing. There was a yoga studio with a hot tub connected to the living room, a commercial-grade kitchen, and a theatre. We continued down a hallway and passed through a heavy oak door into the dining area, which was a spacious room enclosed on all sides. There were several doors on each of the four walls which offered a thrill and a little disorientation to the newly arrived. In the middle sat a long cedar table. "Through that door's the kitchen. Four of 'em are bedrooms, but I don't know who's in where, so we ain't gonna go pokin' around," he said. "One of 'em's a steam room, another is built for massages with candles and smellies and low music, but I can't think which is which," he told me. We settled into our seats at the table set for six. Each setting had a plate, ice water, dinner fork, salad fork, dessert fork, knife and a napkin. A servant came through the kitchen door and spoke before she was even in the room.

"Hola," she said, looking down into a plate stacked high with thin layered bread. She placed it on the table and disappeared. As she left, another one of the doors opened slowly. A cautious head poked out across the threshold. The head belonged to a dirty, loose-moving white man.

"We eatin' soon?" he asked. His eyes were wide and probing. The spirited smell of old cheap weed invited itself past him in the doorway and out into the dining room to join us for dinner. Hardy spoke up.

"Yeah, we usually eat around eight," he said.

"Cool," the baffled looking man shuffled out into the new room with his jeans bunched into the top of his cowboy boots.

"I like that coat," I said.

"Oh, yeah?" Without looking down, he slowly ran his hand over his jacket, checking to see if he was still on his chest. His fingers were covered in mechanical grease and his nails were lined in black soot. "This is an old hand-to-me-down," he said. His head wobbled stiffly on his neck like a plate spinning on a pole and his bulging eyes were set on me.

"Really?" I said.

"Really," he said. The speed of sound is somewhere around seven hundred miles-per-hour. The words shot from his mouth at about fifty-five. His name was Ickie, short for Icarus, and he settled into the bench next to me and put his arms on the table. His faded green sleeves lied like parenthesis around the bright white dinner plate. His story began like the slow rev of a boat motor, but it eventually found its speed.

"No, he's fixin' to die in Spicewood, the guy that gave my buddy this jacket. Got that cancer. All these old military guys are all fucked up from this cancer, y'know. He's one of those guys who, probably twiny years ago, in Spicewood, bought ten acres on a hilltop, man. And he ain't got nothin'. He drug his Winnebago up there. It wouldn't even drive, he had to hook it up and drug it. He bought that land and thought, 'Alright, I'm gonna make out on it someday.' Well, he's gonna die before he ever gets to sell it, y'know. And everybody that comes to look at it, and the tax people, know he's gonna die, and they're just waiting, and they're gonna get a better deal on it. I'm on the outside lookin' in, y'know. That's what they're doing. So, he came, my buddy did, and visit with 'im up in Spicewood. Ain't seen 'im in like twiny years. Military guy said, 'Ah, I ain't gettin' no compensation for my cancer,' y'know. He been waitin' like, fer a long time. Waitin' on a requital. He was tortured in Vietnam. Sleep deprivation, isolation, *star*vation. He told my buddy all this shit's goin' on that no one knows about, dude. He ain't got nothin' to lose, now. Told 'im 'bout the Whitewater deal. All those records were in that deal, in that building. That truck blew up in Oklahoma, but there was a bomb in that frickin' room. They just made it look like it was the truck. Guess who looks like the hero, man? Billiam Clinton, y'know. Comes in, swoops up all the 'ttention, gets the heat off him, right? I mean that's what this military guy in Spicewood says, y'know. I mean I b'lieve 'im. All the sudden this frickin' guy, this frickin' farmer, can go buy all this fertilizer and build a frickin' bomb out of it? That's kinda hard to b'lieve that somebody can go do that, y'know? Yeah. Military guy in Spicewood said they paid that man five-hunerd-thousand dollars to do that. Gave him the bombs. But they went and got 'im anyways then give 'im the death penalty. They set 'im up.

"You remember that, uh, Branch Davidians in Waco? David Koresh? Y'know, they were on, like, a stand-off, for, I don't know, like a week or two, trying to get 'em out of there and all that shit. Then all the sudden one morning the place burned down, that night. It just frickin' burned. Well, that night, during the night, some of those badass military things that hover like a helicopter supposed to came in and just shot that mother fucker up and they blazed off then they torched the bodies.

"That's another thing that military guy told my buddy over there when he come and visit with him. This jacket is his. He just give it to my buddy who give it to me. Crazy, huh? And it's probably the truth. All of it's probably true. Sounds truer than all that other bullshit in these popular frickin' news stories. And the military guy up in Spicewood's gettin' screwed on the whole cancer deal. Agent Orange. He's so fucked up now it don't matter. He ain't got no teeth. It's real rough on you, y'know? Well, he gots false teeth he puts in."

"Right," I said.

A second man wearing camouflaged bibs came out of another one of the bedrooms with an unlabeled mason jar of clear liquor. He went around the table picking up our waters and poured four of them back into the pitcher, then dumped splashes of hooch into the cold sweating glasses.

"Oh, gee, not me," Hardy said. "Luke can have mine."

I was leaning forward with my elbows on the table. My hands were folded together in front of me while I listened to the wide-eyed man. The man in the bibs took Hardy's glass and slid it under my nose. I looked down at it.

Just then, a brown-haired woman spun into the room directly across the table from me. She was wearing muddy hiking boots and a frayed wool cardigan with Mexican stitching embroidered onto the chest. She had a burnt-in tan from years in the sun, and she hugged a hot mug of tea. Behind her was a shorter, much older woman in men's jeans who stood with her hands clasped in front of her waist and her head tilted back, which made her neck look thick and sturdy. Short white hairs scattered out from the edges of her hand-knit wool beanie.

The brown-haired woman made a round of introductions with the untaught decency of a skilled party girl, and the sloped irreverent eyes of a legitimate beatnik hipster. She was the only unsuspicious one in the room.

"Rob and Ickie, I see you've met Hardy and his friend. I'm Sarah, and this is Cookie," she said to me, running her words together like a stoned academic. "We spoke on the tube," she said to me and placed papers and pens on our dinner plates. I looked over at Hardy. He tugged at his straight hair, and never took his eyes off Sarah. "I don't mean to be uncool, but I want to get some of this messiness out of the way before we eat," Sarah said. "In front of you is an agreement."

I picked it up and scanned it, a legitimate legal document.

"It says, what we all already know, that tonight y'all are here to eradicate the black feral hogs from this property and that you will do so confidentially. Rob and Ickie, you were hand-picked by Cookie because she is confident in your skills with a bow." Cookie stood in the corner and nodded. "Luke, you're a friend of Cully's and he's spoken highly of your abilities as an outdoorsman as well."

"Thank you. Um, but what are we signing exactly? Why is this a secret?" I asked.

"It's not a *secret,* like… 'shhh'…it's just that if word got out that we're killing hogs on the ranch, a majority of our clientele wouldn't be too happy. And keeping them happy is why we're here. We have the big hot air balloon weekend coming up next month and it's important attendance is high."

"And they would cancel if they heard we were killing hogs?" I asked. Before she could respond, Ickie spoke up.

"You're bringing balloons here? Fuck them balloons, man. The Japs used balloons to bomb Oklahoma during World War II," Ickie said. "No one ever talks about that."

Sarah got everyone quieted down. "Dripping Dreams attracts nature lovers, seekers, artists, painters," she said then paused. "They come from Austin," she lifted her eyebrows. "And most are transplants from somewhere else before that. They don't get Texas. They require a certain *brand* of nature, and we give it to them. We offer a place of repose and quietness. They don't understand that what y'all are doing here actually minimizes suffering. And we are lucky to have a man of science to oversee the entire operation," she said. Hardy's shoulders bounced with an embarrassed laugh. He stood up and addressed the group.

"Mgay, so, we've been running these spotlighting sessions at measured intervals over the last four years. The main synopsis of my data is that the hog population has shrunk and is on its way to a healthier level since hunting has commenced," he said. Sarah smiled proudly at him like a mother.

"'Cause you killin' 'em," Ickie said plainly.

"Cookie and I believe that death is a perpetual verity of life," Sarah said to him, then turned to me. "But, death without respect is slaughter. So, we ask one thing of you, besides discretion. We request that you ask permission before killing the hogs."

"You called me," Ickie laughed. "Ain't that permission?"

"No, not me," she said, and walked over to him. She caressed both of this cheeks, "I want you to ask permission from the animals." She stood up and spoke to us all. "In whatever way you see fit, in whatever religious or spiritual connection that you maintain with the divine and mystic; recognize your place in the systems of the natural world and ask the hog for its life. Ask her for her meat to nourish you. Ask her for her tirelessness and wit and energy. Ask her for her breath that…"

"Slow down," Rob said, writing violently on his palm with a pen. "I ain't gonna be able to remember all that."

"Yeah, a lot of times these sows'll rush up on yuh quick," Ickie said. "We ain't gone have time to ask 'er *all* that."

"Well, what if one of us ask 'ems while the other's drawing on 'em?" Rob said to his partner.

"Well, I guess that would work if they was only one sow, but mostly they run in packs," Ickie said. "We'd be missin' out on half our hogs if we had to ask 'em all questions."

Rob looked up at and said, "What if we asked 'em all at once, that way we wouldn't be out there rushin' our shots and fergettin' exactly what we're s'posed to be askin' first of all?" We all agreed that would be a good idea and stood in a circle around the oak table holding hands and opened the lines of transmission with the beasts in the night. Since Sarah was the most comfortable communicating across species, we let her do the imploring.

"At Dripping Dreams," she began, "we believe that all beings are drops of water balancing along a string; a string that runs from the beginning, through the present, through our bodies, and into the undeviating future." When she spoke, she stretched every syllable. "When it is time, these beads collide and fall from the string that holds them. Wild sows and piglets we ask you tonight for your blood, for your beating heart, for your…" she went on in that way until it was over.

CHAPTER 3 ...
Spotlighting

The moon was a sliver, and the black Texas sky was cluttered with stars. They almost looked gaudy up there, like a horde of excess. I once worked for a widow in Montana who kept twenty-three dogs. I asked her how she could know twenty-three dogs and love them all. She told me to take the love I had for Cane and divide it by twenty-three. She told me I'd still have enough to fill up my whole heart. Those stars were like that; a dividend wide enough to be cut into twenty-thirds and yet have the power to pop something inside and make me leak a little charm.

The dented white pickup truck creaked slowly along the windswept dirt road. Half-exposed limestone rocks studded the trail and made it a slow, bumpy ride. The hard wind flattened my hood against my cheek but it didn't break through. I had aimed south for warmer weather and still hadn't found it.

Cullom sat in the cab of the pickup, on the passenger side with a notebook in his lap, shining his spotlight out his window, covering the right side of the road. He was giddy like a teenager sneaking out of the house. The two hunters and I stood in the bed. I was in the middle, shining the light out to the left on Ickie's side while Rob, in his camo bibs, was on the right guided by Cullom's light. Riding in the back of the truck felt like an amusement park ride, except it was free, and you got to keep what you killed. Through the sliding rear window, Cullom told me to make sure that I was scanning my entire view to ensure thorough reportage. Cookie drove the truck since she was the only one with the militant patience to hold her foot on the brake for three straight hours. Sarah stayed behind at Casa Simba, because she had some reading to do. A poet friend of hers was coming from Austin in the morning so she needed to review his latest book and think of inventive ways to compliment it. From her sofa, all the killing was out of sight.

"Watch your heads, guys," Cullom whispered through the window as we drove under juniper branches that hung low across the road. The male juniper boughs produced an orange dusty pollen that was so chalky and brittle, if it brushed your cheek, it would leave a deep orange mark like a gash across your face. There was enough pollen in the air already that Ickie, Rob and I were hunting with swollen eyes.

"Here, chunk these out as we go," Cookie said, reaching back through the window. She gave me a handful of store-bought arrowheads. I looked them over in my palm.

"Should I peel the stickers off first?" I asked, through the window.

"Yeah, take them off. The injuns couldn't afford a buck fifty for an arrowhead." So, as we rolled along, I flipped them out the back of the pickup into creek bottoms or walking paths.

On the north side of the hills, the soil was smooth and a little wet beneath our tires, but the dull ruts had our bodies rolling and swaying in tandem like three oak trees joggled in a windstorm. My neck was weak, and the bouncing of the truck rocked my eyes closed while I stood with the light in my gloved hand.

"Keep the light moving," Cullom whispered through the window. I jerked awake and looked at the two men with their compound bows on either side of me.

I saw animals everywhere, but all of the silhouettes I saw in the bushes were symptoms of my sleeplessness. A shrub was a coyote, a boulder was a giant toad, a fallen log was a naked human body, but only briefly. The shapes were ghostly white traces before my eyes could settle on them and straighten it out.

I could handle these hallucinations. They happened a lot while driving with Cane at night, fleeing one city only to have an uglier knotted episode of paranoia when I arrived in the next. A deprived mind will make shortcuts. Vague, ambiguous shapes turn quickly into recognizable figures because they are more useful and easier to classify. Our brains work quickly with things they recognize. Patterns simplify a random and confusing world. When blocks surround us, we can toy with them. Make decisions. Stay safe.

When my spotlight's beam hit the eyes of a mother hog, they glowed with a striking green luminescence. The animal froze in suspicion. The eyes seemed to float against the black backdrop.

Cullom tapped Cookie on the shoulder, "Stop. Stop. Stop."

She stomped the brakes tight. My hands went down to catch myself on the roof of the truck, which aimed the spotlight straight into the cab and off the rearview mirror.

"Jaysus fucking Christ!" Cookie yelled. She was blinded. She buried her face in her soiled yellow mittens and let her foot off the brake. While she rubbed the light out of her eyes, the truck crawled off the road.

"Cookie, the brakes!" Cullom yelled, and we thumped straight into a juniper tree, which threw Ickie, Rob and me onto the roof of the cab. Sheets of pollen fell on us like flour from a sifter.

"Son of a buck," Cullom said, cranking up his passenger side window. The hogs ran off. We all collected ourselves, and Cookie backed the truck up onto the road.

"Since we're stopped...Luke throw me the hippo feet," Cookie said, hopping down out of the truck with her short legs. All around our feet in the truck bed was the assorted trash and tools and farm equipment that cluttered the beds of all ranch trucks in Texas. There were arrows, twisted barbwire, beer cans [empty], beer cans [full], a caulk gun, channel-lock pliers with grease-stained rubber handles, chain, chain-link fencing, a chainsaw chain [no chainsaw], a come-along, a cooler [full], a gas can, a hatchet, a ladder, liquid nail, lumber, machine parts, nails, assorted pipes of various lengths, pulleys, riffle cartridges, rivets, saw blades, screws, a sheet of tin, a shovel, a speed square, springs, a ten-pound sledge. I reached down between Ickie's feet and grabbed a matching set of large metal molds, almost like cookie cutters, in the shape of animal feet, with leather straps and buckles hanging from them. I handed them down to Cookie.

"No those are rhinos," she said, handing them back. "Four toes." She pointed impatiently. I found the pair she wanted and gave them to her. She walked a few yards into the brush and strapped them onto her boots. She walked with long strides in front of the truck. Like an aging sasquatch with bad knees, she crossed through headlights slowly, her old bones struggling to move the heavy plates. Once she made it to the other side, she bent down and unstrapped the buckles, then tossed them into the truck, almost breaking my ankle. They crashed into the other tools in the bed, and the sound made my heart jump. I thought we'd never see a boar with all the noise we were making. But, there's a reason Texas has such relaxed laws on killing wild boar. They're thick with them. Only a quarter-mile or so down the road we came upon another pack. This time they didn't spook, and the hunters laid into them.

Ickie and Rob could both operate a bow. They slung arrows, one after another, spraying blood and sticking piglets to the ground. The truck crept along, following the scattering hogs. I watched Ickie work. He drew the string back with his right hand and pointed the index finger of his left quietly at the target. He shared a private, singular moment with each beast, like a child pointing his finger through a car window at passing pedestrians.

When every hog was either dead or out of bow range, the men jumped from the truck. Their breath steamed.

"I stuck that gnarly boar by the stump, dropped him, then put one through the big gilt, and the sow ran off to the left in them cactus."

"I pulled up on one but he was running at me ass-backward, so I didn't get a shot off on'm, so I spun and stuck a little one to the ground." That animal was still croaking and bleeding out. "Then I knocked another arruh, put *it* through a boar, and he's lying under that mesquite."

"Aye, Yankee, go find that gilt," Rob said to me. "I thumped her in the hips, she ain't gon' be far. Might have to finish 'er off with tha hatchet." I jumped out of the truck and slid the handle of the hatchet through my belt loop. Then I made my way into the pasture to follow the blood trail. The streaks of blood on the blades of grass were glassy and thick in the harsh white spotlight. I walked cautiously from one drop to the next, looking forward, imagining the waddling pig as she tripped panicked through the grass. The blood trail led into a patch of junipers — she was confused and in pain. Wounded animals will try to find tight cover, or water if they can. In the thicket, the blood was harder to spot. I'd find a splash of blood, barely visible in the dirt, and follow my line forward but come upon nothing, so I'd have to double back and take a different path. The circling back wore on my already hazy mind. I returned to the same small speck three times because I couldn't find any new blood. The speckle was a perfect red circle on a fallen live oak leaf. Live oaks have football-shaped leaves that they can lose rapidly in February to make way for regrowth. On the fourth try, I went about a hundred feet to the north without finding another drop. Worried that if I went any farther, I'd never find my live oak leaf again, I turned back. But just then, I spotted a heavy smear of blood high on a mesquite branch. I looked back toward the road and could barely see the headlights of the pickup truck a few hundred yards away. Ickie and Rob's flashlights crisscrossed the pasture on the other side looking for more lost hogs. I stooped under the smear of blood and entered another, even more dense patch of heavy green juniper boughs covered in orange dusty pollen. Stepping over cactus, crouching and ducking through the soft needles, I lost the road. In every direction, there were streaks of blood high up in the trees. I got spun around and disoriented chasing her. I stumbled forward with my head low, and stepped between two tight cactus bushes. I ducked under a thin bony branch and staggered into a large flat clearing in the underbrush. And there it stood — a lone imitation. A towering leafless live oak tree, every inch dripping with dense black oil. My spotlight glinted off the ominous steaming trunk as I approached it. The black oil ran in heavy streaks down the furrows in the bark. From within the chaotic limbs came the smell of the hot innards of an animal. I stood under the tree, fixed to the earth, swaying. Oil dripped from the tips of the branches and landed in black globules that rolled in the sand. My head was cocked back, my throat white and exposed. A force pulled my body up into the tree. The spotlight hung loosely in my hand, aimed at the golden sand.

As I rose, the circle of light back on the ground dilated like a cloud of rocket exhaust. My feet were lowered on a slippery limb, thirty feet in the air. In front of me, buried in a nexus of branches, sat a bright white bow, tied in a ribbon on a thin crooked black bough. Satin. White satin, or silk. I rested the flashlight on a thick limb and plucked the band off the twig. There was oil on my hand. I slid the warm liquid sinfully between my fingertips, then slowly pulled the tips of the ribbon until the knot dissolved in my hands. When I looked up, I was on the ground, and the tree was gone.

"She's fucking dying, Porter!" I spun around, and the G.I. was yelling at me from his knees on the other side of the clearing. A middle-aged woman was lying on her back across his lap in street clothes, blood covering her forehead and hands. Her legs were crushed and contorted, and they lied unnaturally in the dirt. I walked slowly across the clearing and kneeled over her.

I asked the G.I., "Why did you bring her here?" Before he could answer, the woman twitched and writhed in the soil and was too hurt to notice me. The nametag on her mint green nurse's scrubs read, Anette. Gently, I lifted her head and tied the soiled white ribbon into her black hair. Then I placed my palm against her cheek. The oil disappeared from my fingertips. The sound of the pickup truck's horn ripped through the trees, and I knew I had to get back or they'd come looking for me.

CHAPTER 4 ...

Steam

The next day, I went to Casa Simba looking for Sarah. I needed cash and thought the hot air balloon weekend might create a need for labor. The cook told me I'd find her in the steam room. When I said I'd come back some other time, she smirked and insisted that it would be fine. Sarah took meetings in there almost weekly. I walked the halls hesitantly and reached a thick oak door that was warm and sweating. I knocked.

"Come in," she said. I looked both ways down the hall and turned the handle. Steam rushed over me. An involuntary laugh lifted her words.

"Close the door, soldier, you're going to trip the smoke alarm." The only thing I could see, besides the floor, were her toes curling as she watched me grapple with the fog. When I opened my mouth to breath, the steam brushed over my tongue. I could feel the heat against my eyeballs. "I'm glad you've decided to start enjoying yourself," she said. "Take your shirt off. Your pants, too. People in pants tend to be anxious. I've seen it happen." I could still only see her feet. "Here, sit." I heard her wet palm pat the wooden bench.

I squinted while I slid my pants off, folded them, and set them, along with my boots, outside in the hallway.

"I'm actually here to talk to you," I said, closing the door quickly behind me.

"Oh, fantastic," she said. As I stood in the middle of the steaming box with the hot coals burning behind me, her shape started to appear. Her tanned, smooth knees were only a few feet from mine, and when she saw that my eyes were beginning to adjust, she crossed her legs. There was a bluebonnet embroidered into the corner of the white towel that was wrapped tightly around her thighs. She wore another towel around her head, holding her hair up off her neck.

"I was wondering if there was any work to be done around here," I said. "I don't know if Hardy has told you, but I'm sort of a traveling handyman. I live in that van with tools and the dog."

"I love that," she said. "No ties. You just ride around looking for things that interest you. And you chose Dripping Dreams."

"I landed in Texas looking for warmer weather. I'm from up north, but I've been traveling the country for a year or so now." The process of selling myself to every spinster entrepreneur and landowning widow across America had gotten old, but my pitch still sparkled and had the same effect, especially on women like Sarah. They loved having a young drifter on the grounds. Some kid they can tell their friends about, brag, giggle. "I could help set up for the event this weekend," I said. "Maybe cook the carrot dogs...wrangle a stray balloon, I don't know."

"Hmmm," she tilted her head. A wet piece of hair stuck to her forehead and the rest fell to the side. "There *is* a lot to be done, but Cookie handles most of it. She doesn't work well with others. Especially men."

"I mean, I'm not looking to take anyone's job. I can do some carpentry, plumbing, electrical work. I've worked with animals."

"To be honest I'd love to use you, but I just can't pay you. Cash is rare as rain around here. And I'm sorry about the cold. March will warm this place up."

"I can't stick around through March on no money. It's hard to believe that you don't have any cash. Looking at the place, I'd think you could afford to hire some help," I said.

"The land is worth millions, the houses are worth millions, but the business is worth shit," she said. "I inherited the land from my father and I'm trying to make something of it."

"Did he run cattle?" I asked. I sat down on the bench next to her and felt the hot wood press and stick to my back. I breathed in deeply. Her face looked like it did the night before, easy and cryptic at the same time. The fog softened it around the edges.

"He started an oil development company in Midland in the 60s. That's where he made his money. We did have cattle and horses, though, just for fun. My father always wanted to fit in with the ranchers. I was the kind of girl who got a pony when she wanted one. I went to the best private schools in Dallas but dropped out of college to globe-trot, kind of like what you're doing."

"Kind of. I bet your oil drilling daddy didn't like that," I said.

"Not exactly. And he didn't actually drill at all. What he did was follow these oil companies all around the desert, and buy the mineral rights to the properties *next to* the land that they drilled. If the oil company hit big, the price of the neighboring land shot way up, then my father would sell. He had an old Princeton pal who went into business with him and got just as rich but they had a falling out. I don't know why I'm telling you all this." She chuckled, wiped the sweat from her forehead then put her hand on the bench between us and rested her weight on it. "The steam makes me a little dotty. It's the closest to drunk I get anymore. It's almost dream-like. Just dehydration, I guess."

"I know what you mean. Sometimes it feels like you're dreaming when you're wide awake," I said, looking at the floor. The first bead of sweat stung as it poked through the skin on my forehead. "Sometimes you dream something that feels so familiar. Like you aren't sure if you're seeing it for the first time or the hundredth."

"Yes," she said. I could tell I was about to be pulled

into something poetic. "There's a vision I keep in my mind. Or, it keeps me, I guess," she said. "It's soothing. It's a running dream. You know, the ones where you run across your entire hometown and never get tired? But this isn't a town, it's an endless field. There's no beginning or end. I'm just there running. My little feet are pumping, and they're carrying me across a pasture. There is a pressure in my legs that grows steadily, and I welcome it like a throbbing that spreads and deepens from the inside. It's as if there are no strides, only an unbroken sense of motion beneath me. It burns uninterrupted and unnaturally fast. The ground moves under me, silently, just a blurred plane of unruly grass. Wind rips past my ears and I'm not running from anything. I'm moving toward a fat red sun that sits on the western tree line." She was staring at the coals in the pit. "I can see the pink and orange sky unrolling the light outward from the middle like infinity stretching its arms. Then, the field dips and I'm facing downhill, which encourages speed. With speed, the burning beneath me intensifies, and so does the satisfaction that comes with it. The funny part is, I couldn't tell you if the dream is even mine." She broke her stare and turned to me. "When I was a little girl in West Texas my sister described that vision to me. So, it must be hers. Stories will do that. They linger somewhere inside of me, alive like an organism."

"It doesn't have to be yours for you to feel it," I said. "We're all borrowing when we dream. Borrowing scenes, borrowing faces, then fastening them to emotions. Fluid, stupid, everyday emotions. Do you know what a potter wasp is?" I asked. She shook her head but her foggy eyes never left hold of mine. "They're these wasps that build their nests out of mud and saliva. Little brown clay nests. You've seen them. They take mud: the raw stuff of the earth, and inject themselves into it and make a home. Make their safety," I said.

"I bet you've got a big imagination," she said.
"So big it hurts," I said.

"You've had what, twenty-something years to grow one?" she asked.

"Twenty-three." I leaned forward and rested my elbows on my thighs and breathed in the heat. I watched sweat fall from my nose, between my limp hands and land on the hot wooden floor. She took the towel off her head and laid it around the back my neck. I could smell her when she leaned in, but I couldn't feel her the way you can normally feel the heat of a body against yours. The room robbed us of that.

"You know, when you were describing those nests, I was picturing some big momma wasp flying back and forth between her home and the hardware store. A little insect hardware store, just like people have, under some forgotten upturned wheelbarrow. Bugs fly in through automatic sliding doors into an air-conditioned warehouse and isles and isles of mud sit on shelves. Any flavor of mud you could imagine is available: sandy river mud, North American brown silt, coastal saltwater mud, even good rich, nitrogen-infused rainforest sludge. Ladybugs fly around wearing aprons with their names written across the chest, asking the customer bugs if they need any help. Bees fly in, asking for pollen. Termites meander through isles of ragged wood, just splinters of each kind."

We sat in silence for a moment. "Little Mexican bugs in the parking lot looking for work," I said.

"Kinda like you," she said, nudging me with her freckled shoulder.

"I've worked with plenty of Mexicans and I've never seen a white boy that was able to keep up, myself included."

"So, you just float around fixing fences and busted toilet seats? You don't take pictures? You don't write? A professional traveler that just…travels."

"No, I can't take a good picture. Shaky hands. Plus, seeing the thing is worth it enough. I don't need a picture. If I need to see a place again, I go back."

"I bet your lonely," she said. "When I was young traveling around Europe, I hated the loneliness. I'd sleep with random men just for the company. Sometimes we didn't even speak the same language. There must be something you do for fun," she said.

"I like to fly-fish," I said. "And, every once in a while, I'll pick up a hitchhiker and kill him with a hammer."

"Sounds messy," she said.

"I have a tarp."

"If you like to fish you ought to go to Castell. Fish the Llano River," she said. "It's only an hour or so from here. There's a cute little store there that's just your speed. I'll bet they can put you to work, too. I knew the owner years ago. Spent a few wild nights with him on the river. Randy. He died a year ago. Heart attack in the doggy-style position. The girl was about twenty years younger than him. She said he finished then died with a smile on his face."

"Maybe I'll check it out," I said.

She uncrossed her legs and reached forward and grabbed my hand. She pulled it back towards her and held it in her lap. When I turned to looked at her, I could see up her towel. She wasn't hiding anything. It was dense and dark between her legs. Thick pubic hair spilled down the inside of her thighs. I looked up at her face. There was a wasp mounted on her tanned cheek. It pumped its sternum back and forth.

"I have to go," I said. "I can't work for free, and I have to buy dog food," I said. I pulled my hand away from her and stood up too quickly. The room went black and the deafening sound of wasp wings hummed in my head.

"Are you okay?" Sarah asked. I reached behind me for the door but instead rested my hand in the coals. I shouldered the door open and found my boots in the hallway. I threw on my clothes and walked the quarter mile from Casa Simba to the van where Cane waited, curled up in the passenger seat. I started the engine and aimed for the gate.

CHAPTER 5 ...
Arrival in Castell

My phone cut out somewhere around Hico. The rest of the navigation was on instinct and road signs. I knew the general direction I needed to go, so, when I came on a chance to turn here or there, I followed my gut. I was headed west on Highway 29 when I saw a sign just past a dried creek crossing. Hand written on a piece of scrap sheet metal was a simple direction– "Turn for Castell General Store" – written in black paint with sloppy male handwriting and an arrow pointing south down Farm to Market Road 2768. It didn't say how far. I looked over at Cane. He was staring into my lap where bits of scrambled egg and bacon from my breakfast taco had fallen into my seat. I reached down below my crotch and dug out the soft warm egg and bacon bits. I held the food under his nose. He gently bit down with his incisors and plucked the breakfast from my fingertips then jerked his head up toward the ceiling and tossed it into his mouth.

On the two-lane asphalt road, we sped past a pasture feeding eight or ten head of longhorns, a few of which looked up lethargically at our odd colored van. They were odd colored themselves. An orange bull with crisp white patches navigated the tips of his horns gracefully in and out of a barbed wire fencing like a seamstress with a needle. He then ducked and swung them with precision around the haunches of a white steer. The land was doing to me what it did to the Germans in the 1840s, and to the Prussian and Russian settlers before them, and to the Comanche before them, and the Apache before them. It was gripping me with its harshness and charming me into submission.

Inside the van, the air was stale. I hadn't noticed how or when, but it had gotten hot. I cranked down the window, spinning the handle in the door, and felt the wind slice through the cab. I took off my cap and tossed it on the dash. It settled sideways under the windshield. It was a warm healthy wind that smelled like grass and bark and asphalt. A hard right turn slowed our progress, and as we wound back to the left, I saw the Llano River laid out below us. The water was clean and cobalt blue. It looked like an uncorked lazy pool tucking and spinning softly between pink granite boulders the size of cars. A low slab bridge offered passage a few feet above the shallow water's surface and wasn't resistant or averse to the river, but instead looked to be part of it. In places, the concrete slab was supported naturally by the giant stones that sat stoic and still in the water. The hunks of Precambrian granite were massive, a matte pinkish grey color. Every one of the boulders had a soothing shape to it, bulbous with soft rounded edges and cracks. They pacified me; giant balls of tortilla dough to toy with in my mind. You would have thought that there was a design to them, especially if you're the type whose spirit is pulled outdoors by rushing water and dirt.

Cane whimpered with excitement when he saw the water and kneaded the seat cushion with his paws. There was a muddy flat patch off to the side of the road before the bridge. Another scrap metal sign with the same black handwriting read, "Parking Courtesy of Castell General Store." There was one vehicle in the small brown patch at the edge of the water. It was a truck fixed up like it belonged to an outdoorsman with extra gas and water jugs fastened to the roll bar in the bed. Hand over hand, I slowly turned the van into the mud patch and rolled to the opposite side of the parking lot away from the truck. In the country, you give people their space if you can, and you don't burden anyone with your role, at least not a stranger, so I put the van in park and left the diesel engine running. I wasn't sure of my next move. The dog and I got out and walked over to the clear water. I squatted down next to the edge, trying to get as close as I could to the bright, reflective current. My boot pressed down on the sandy lip and dipped into the water. The river dragged a thin ripple around my toe. I felt the sun pressing on my neck for the first time in months. Looking at the river, I understood what came before. What had to have come before. In that moment, I believed in the promise of the heat on my shoulder. It was a reminder that spring will always return and that as long as the math remains unbroken, biology will keep allowing for wildflowers and mesquite trees and Guadalupe bass.

For a Northerner, traveling south to chase this gift is greedy, in a way. We are supposed to put our chins in our palms and wait for the sun to come to us. That's what everyone back home did, everyone that didn't make it out or never wanted to leave in the first place. Back home, there was pride in sitting through the seasons, waiting for lakes to unfreeze, waiting for the baseball grass to turn sticky and green, waiting for lawnmowers to cough back to life, waiting for that first sunburn to brighten your nose. It feels like you've earned spring if you've waited for it. Waited so long that you've almost given up hope on it ever returning. But I didn't need to wait. I had a yellow van that brought the sun to me.

A man stood in the middle of the river, waist deep among the boulders, looking down through the water below him into the abstract stone-colored bottom. It must have been the owner of the truck. The man was sturdy and useful looking. His shoulders were thick and his rounded forearms held up his rolled shirtsleeves. With his elbow fixed in the air, he pulled a fly rod back and forth past his ear. The yellow line above his head was perfectly flat, parallel with the surface of the water. He was patient and rhythmic. With each pass, the line lengthened as if it was gathering invisible nylon out of the air above him. One more cast and he let the line fall atop the racing water.

I dipped my cupped hands into the river and brought it up to my mouth. It was cold and clean. On both banks were slanted trees, leafless but beginning to bud, their branches pointing downstream. Among the pale limbs that hovered just above the silt, thick grasses and coarse shrubbery pushed upward. Tall wildflowers with thin red pedals on long stems nodded elegantly above the grass. I stood and walked upstream along the bank, watching the river change. In the pastures around the stream grew Texas yellowstars, bluebonnets and orange Indian paintbrushes. Cane sniffed up and down the hill that shouldered the water. I eventually sat down against a piece of driftwood. For the first time in over a year, I fell fast into a dark dreamless stagnant sleep.

When I woke up, it was dark, but the air was still warm. Country music bellowed across the water from the bridge. The fly fisherman was gone. The dog had been sleeping next to me, but the bombast woke him, too. I got to my feet and swiped the sand and small bone-colored stones off my cheek. Another buggy ripped past and made its way up the hill on the other side of the river. I watched it climb behind the budding trees and that's when I noticed the Castell General Store for the first time. The ATV parked in front of the yellow building a few hundred yards past the bridge. The Store sat on top of the hill. In the daylight, it was tough to see through the trees, but at night it glowed, lit up like a circus tent, the only show in town, the only proof of a town at all.

When I got back to the van, I realized it had run out of fuel. There was a voicemail on my phone from my sister, Marla. Cellphone service was spotty, just the way I liked it. It made it easier to dodge appointments and life back home, a life that only existed to me through my phone. It was a Thursday night and the full moon was so bright, I walked across the bridge with a shadow. I could hear the black water suck between the stones and rush under my feet.

As I climbed up the hill, it became clear that the Store *was* Castell, and Castell *was* the Castell General Store. There was nothing but a few historical homes spread along the street and a church in a field connected to the modern world only by a snaking sandy driveway. A post office with chipping white paint was down the street, too. Across from the Store, there was an old barn suspended in a slow patient collapse. Warped rotten wood held up a rusted tin roof. Plastic kayaks spilled out of a large doorless doorway at the front of the half-fallen building. Life jackets and paddles were piled up against the corner. A hand painted sign leaning against a nearby tree said in the same hapless human font, "DON'T STEAL. YOU ARE ON CAMERA."

The road that crossed the river intersected with another highway, County Road 152. Most small towns have a speed limit, some even have a stop sign, but I didn't see any in Castell. Drivers were slowed by their own curiosity and the curvature of the road.

Some trucks were parallel parked in front of the porch, others lined up near the Store's smoker and barbecue pits. The truck belonging to the fisherman was among them.

On the porch, two old men in cowboy hats talked loudly at one another. One wore a white hat; the other wore black. It was still early enough in the season for felt. They were smoking cigarettes and didn't notice me on the unlit road, but when I was in the light of the porch, they both looked but didn't nod. Had we been in trucks passing on the highway, I would have gotten the little finger wave from the top of the steering wheel, but in person all I got was ignored.

"And, she had too much leather under her throat?" the man in the black hat asked.

"Too much leather," the man in the white hat confirmed.

"And little bitty shoulders?" black hat asked.

"Little bitty ones."

"And that's why I didn't sell her?"

"Decided not to."

"You didn't sell her because she had too much leather under her throat and little bitty shoulders?"

"That's raht."

"You thought you'd keep her?"

"Raht."

I walked in through the front door. It was red and the latch barely worked. It was bright and loud and friendly, full of cowboy hats and snakeproof boots. There were about fifteen people standing around the bar, or sitting at mismatched tables with mismatched chairs holding matching bottles of beer. Some southern voice sang through a small speaker behind the bar, trying to convince me of something. Beer bottles clanked and worn out voices laughed. It was a warm atmosphere in a strangely decorated room, and you got the feeling it wasn't strangely decorated on purpose. It felt thrown together. Not eclectic, just someone's best effort.

The shelves were somewhat stocked. Items that visitors to the hill country might have needed sat unorganized and spread out. Light groceries, batteries, things like that. These artifacts of all variety and age, once on the shelf, sat alongside each other for years. Thing next to thing. One shelf held a stack of shotgun shells, only dove-load, only 20-gauge, next to eight different types of salsa, (no chips) next to pitching washers, next to an opened box of automotive fuses, next to baby bottles, only two, next to a stack of car batteries covered in dust, next to a pyramid of Velveeta cheese bumper enough to feed the Russian Army, next to half a dozen toothbrushes, new but unpackaged standing in a plastic cup like a bouquet of childish color.

I walked over to the corner of the shelf which hid the fishing tackle. Trout eggs in small soiled mason jars, leads still in the packaging, plastic bobbers, and wooden lures from the sixties sat in faded blue and red wrappers. The packaging around the bobbers had a picture of a boy on it. He was barefoot with wet blue jean bottoms rolled above the ankle. He held a cane pole and wore a yellow straw hat. Fishing and boyhood will be forever tied in the American memory, secured tightly with a simple overhand knot. It's cute to wonder about the past sometimes. You wonder how fads could bloom and die in a pastime like sport fishing, but they inevitably do, I guess. If you compared the old tackle at the Store to the gear you buy today, you see how it's been improved on. Fishermen are just as susceptible to the promise of progress as any other group, no matter how pure they claim their pursuit is, and no matter that the fish haven't changed.

"You should go into town if you're looking for tackle," I heard someone say behind me. I turned and it was the man I'd seen in the river. He still had his thermal sleeves rolled up to his elbows but his rubber waders had been replaced with a pair of starched Wranglers and some laceless boots.

"Just looking around," I said.

"Most of this stuff, Randy had in his garage, or it was sitting in someone's shed and he bought it off them for a song. Like these old bobbers sat in Glenny's basement soaking in dry time until he died a few years ago and somehow, they ended up at the Store."

"Randy was the owner of the Store?"

"Yeah, he started this place. It was across the street back then, behind the post office. When it came to the fishing gear, or anything on these shelves, really, if you wanted to know the price, you had to ask Randy and watch his eyes while he imagined a number. He might take the lure out of your hand and fiddle with it...feed you some bullshit about how it's rare. Then he'd just give it to you for free. Most of it is only good to a collector at this point. No good for fishing," he said.

"You knew him?"

"Yeah, everyone knew him. He was the reason for this place. He brought Castell back to life."

"There isn't much else around here," I said. I looked over the man's shoulder and saw the bartender glance up at us while she wiped the counter. She turned around and slid the refrigerator door open behind her and grabbed a beer, opened it, and set it on the counter right in front of Ickie. I told the fisherman that it was nice talking to him, but that I was going to get a beer and see a friend. Ickie had picked up his bottle and was standing in a t-shirt he'd cut the sleeves off of. One hand was holding the beer in front of him, the other hand was tucked in his jean pocket and his jeans were tucked into his boots. He stood there, his face locked into one of the only two positions it knew; wide eyes, mouth slightly agape, head perched forward, leading with the nose. I walked up to him and he didn't react at all, but to drink his beer.

"What's goin' on, dude?" he asked plainly as if he'd expected to see me there.

"Not much," I said, strangely eager and hopeful for something to happen. I turned to face the party like he was, both my hands in my pockets.

"Jennifer gotcha beer," he said, as the bartender set a fresh one on the counter next to me and gave me a professional smile, a toothpick in her mouth. Jennifer, on the night I first met her, she was wearing a baseball cap with a patch on the front that said, "Twisted Bitch Cattle Company." I told her thanks and smiled.

Ickie poked his head in between mine and the bartender's. "You drive the banana van?" he asked, and with that, his face changed into the second of its two arrangements. A smile. This look was, for the most part, is exactly the same as the first. The only difference between his intense stare and his smile was that his teeth were exposed and his bulging eyes pinched at the corners. It gives the impression that everything in the world falls into two categories, things that baffle him, and things that amuse him. He flips back and forth between the two expressions with no transition, like a picture book where a pulled tab exposes the dinosaur's teeth.

"Yeah, it's parked across the river," I said. "I fell asleep in the sand earlier."

"Right on. You smoke?"

"Yeah," I started rolling cigarettes years before in Galway, where tobacco taxes are high and the poets can only afford the roll-your-own. I fell in love with one of them once. A poet. She was ten years older than me and her short black hair was wet with Irish rain when she taught me to roll them loosely so the leaf could breathe when I breathed. With her, I felt brave and satisfied using rare words in conversation. Though that isn't bravery, and if stories matter to you, you never feel wholly proud of the words you choose to fill them with.

"Let's go," he said and we headed back out to the porch. "Howerduhyou?" he asked, closing the bar door behind him.

"Twenty-three," I said.

"You like the Gen'ral Store, huh?"

"Yeah, it seems cool," I said.

"It generally ain't got shit you're looking for on the shelves," he said. "Ain't about what's on the shelves, man."

"I'll start looking elsewhere then," I said.

"Twiny-three, huh? You're same age as my son. He's in frickin', uh, Flagstaff, frickin' snowboardin' and shit. He got a little van like you, found a little niche like this up there where people like 'im and he's workin'. Got 'im managing all this shit. Rentin' out, uh, outdoor equipment and shit. Taking people out into the woods 'cause they don't know where the fuck they're goin' and he does. A guide.

"Right."

"He's eatin' it up. He travels kinda like how you're doin' but with a girl. Whenever they was here workin' on a vineyard, it was hot as shit in the fuckin' summer. He said he found this job in Oregon up there on a ranch. Said, 'We wanna go up there and do that,' I said, 'Well fuck, take off and do it.' So, about three weeks later he calls me up and goes, 'Man, Dad, what they got us doin' is we're growin' freakin' weed, y'know.' Ahuh, 'They got us stationed out in this frickin' primitive area watering these plants all day in this cabin. And they're bringin' us supplies.' I'm like dude they're settin' you up, they're doin' it illegal. He says, 'No, it's legal.' So anyway, that's what he did. And my family is like — you know how families are —'Your son's gettin' high.' I'm like, 'Yeah he's fuckin' gettin' high, y'know, shit.' Ahuh."

"So he's in Flagstaff or Oregon?"

"Both, man, er, fuck, I mean, Flagstaff," he said, blowing out his smoke, "Oregon, then Flagstaff. Couple years back he went to live with my mom, y'know, his grandma, and she caught 'im with weed and frickin' came down on 'im, almost booted him out and shit. Anyway, when he got up to Oregon, him and his girlfriend are growing this weed in this little cabin. They took a picture of it for their Christmas card. And they got fuckin' stacks of it, man. And they got bongs sittin' on the table. Took a picture with their arms out, MERRY CHRISTMAS. Ahuh. He sent it to everybody. Yeah, he's a cool dude, man. He loved it over there. You should look into Oregon. And Flagstaff, man."

"My daughter is over in Idaho. She's going to Idaho State to be a painter. I was fixin' to split and go up there 'cause her boyfriend's givin' her a hard time'n shit. She's a tomboy. I saw her two years ago — tomboy. Converse shoes, long sleeve shirt. She got with this little hippie guy, she's all in love with 'im and shit." He pulled out his phone and started poking at it with his thumb.

"I heard Idaho is beautiful," I said.

"Oh, it's fuckin' great, man. I didn't really like her boyfriend, but I thought well fuck that's cool, he loves her and he ain't gonna fuck around or nothin' or anything. Well now she's leavin' 'im. On New Year's Eve she's like, 'I'm leavin'

Malcom, and I need money for an apartment.' Well, this is what she looks like now, she got over all that tomboy shit." He turned his phone toward me and showed me a close-up picture of a college-aged girl with blonde dreadlocks. You could tell she took the picture herself. She was standing on a snowy hill wearing a colorful scarf and snow cap. Her skin was peachy and hazy and monochromatic. She had lizard blue eyes. Ickie couldn't tell because he was from a different generation, and because he was a diesel mechanic, and because he was always stoned, but she had used a filter on the picture, the ones meant to hide imperfections and enhance the pretty colors of a girl's face and to convince their daddies that they're over all that tomboyishness.

"Are those mountains? It looks like mountains in the background there," I said.

"Oh, she's an outdoors person. She's got a dog. Says, 'I don't need no frickin' body.' Well she grew up with my son doin' the same shit he did. She's three years younger than her brother. She's down to hang with him. So, she's out kayaking, climbin' and shit. She loves hangin' with her brother, but they're long ways away now."

"Yeah that's tough," I said.

"The rest of my family never went nowhere, I tole my kids, 'Here's a grand o' money, fuckin put gas in your car and don't get in trouble and call me every day or two, and frickin' go. And they found places where they're doin' good. If you got a mind, you can do it. There's a whole world out there, I'm sure. People get stuck in their own little world and a lot of times you start hanging with the wrong people and you can't leave, or you don't think you can. That's it. A lot of people don't think they can leave. All you need's five-hunerd bucks, pshhhewwww, shoot out there somewhere, see what happens." He put both his hands up by his head, his cigarette wedged in one of them, and cocked his wrists and pointed forward with his index fingers. An old mechanic's fingers never seem to fully straighten out. "I tole 'em, y'know, your car breaks down somewhere it could be the biggest blessin' you ever had. That's like my daughter, she frickin' went up there, tryin' to find a place, all they had was twelve hunerd dollars for an apartment, I was like fuck there's gotta be something else. Look around. Just go to the frickin' coffee shop and ask around 'cause people don't like postin' shit. So, she did, and she ended up with these ex-military guys, they're like sixty-five, seventy years old, and they got this big fuckin' house. There's five of 'em, and they had one more room. So, she's livin' with these freakin' old men, and they fix her car, they take care of her freakin' ass. They're lookin' out after her. I said, I told you, fuck, y'know. Now her boyfriend is textin' her all fuckin' day, and she's trying to break up with 'im. He's probably gonna come fuckin' find 'er, come knock on 'er door. But she got them badass dudes livin' there, so I don't have to drive up there to freakin' whip his dude's ass. I said, 'You figured it out sweetheart.'"

"I guess she did," I said.

When we went back inside, I ordered another beer and asked Jennifer, the bartender, if there was anywhere I might be able to park my van for the night.

"I was planning on fly fishing in the morning, and I want to stay nearby."

"You can park it here, behind the Store," she said. The place was emptying out, and she was wiping down the glass door of the refrigerator. "We have RVs back here all the time. Pull it around in the grass. It's plenty private."

I told her thanks and offered some money, but she wouldn't take it.

"If you want to pay, you can go to the RV park, if you want to stay for free, you come to the Store," she said. I put my money back in my wallet.

CHAPTER 6 ...
Gotta Stay Skeeeny

The next morning, the heavy rain that beat on my van and had me wide-eyed well before the sun came up. It lasted for hours and I knew I wasn't going to be able to fish, the wind would have tormented my fly. The night before, Jennifer had told me that she'd be opening the Store around nine, and that I was welcome to come over when I was done fishing and ready for lunch. I turned the stove on, opened the air vent, and made some eggs and coffee. I sat and smoked a cigarette while the droplets drummed on the roof. When I couldn't take any more of the boredom, I poked my head out of the van and looked up, squinting. I ran through the heavy wind, across the lawn, around to the front of the building and up onto the porch. When I walked in through the front door, the place was empty besides Jennifer behind the bar counting receipts from the night before.

"Heyyyy, you catch anything?" she said enthusiastically, looking quickly back down at her work.

"I never went out. The rain's too heavy. I couldn't even get the dog out of the van."

"Ahhhh," she said, with a full throat, her eyebrows lifted high. It was a forced laugh, but no less charming than a real one. "Does he usually go fishing with you?"

"Yeah he'll sit there on the bank and watch. Sometimes I'll toss him a perch to eat," I said.

"So, you have nothing to do all day?" she asked.

"Just watching the storm," I said.

"We get a few of these every spring. Rain's dangerous this part of Texas. Seems like it's been getting worse these last five years."

"Texans don't believe in climate change," I said, teasing her. I quickly regretted getting political and felt embarrassed.

"There's plenty around here that needs to be done, if you want to work," she said.

"I figured you might have something for me to do."

"Since Randy died, I can't find any help around here. I'm the head bitch and I only got two hands."

"What do you need done?"

"Cleaning house," she said. She grabbed her opened package of beef jerky off the cash register and lead me into the back room. "This is all I eat any more," walking ahead of me, she flipped the clear plastic bag back over her shoulder. The desiccated meat rustled dustily in the pouch. "One meal a day. Gotta stay skeeeny. Keeps these men coming back."

The room, which was large — the ceiling was about twenty feet tall — had two garage doors that opened to the side of the building, and it was packed with junk. Entertaining junk, I thought. Cool old stuff, useful and manly. A walk-in refrigerator took up one part of the room, and there were storage shelves for dry goods, but besides that, every inch of the floor was crammed with the useless clutter of an old man.

"I want this all organized," she swept her hand across it all like a priest blessing a hundred foreheads. Then, she dug her painted fingernails into the bag of jerky and put a piece between her teeth. Half of it was still hanging out of her mouth when she talked.

"All this shit is just in my way. A lot of it came from Randy's when he passed and I want it gone. Anything you think is worth keeping, we can keep, but organize it. But, like this," she pointed to an old golf bag, that was tucked in between a few boxes, "no one will ever use this. His kids came and got what they wanted, but the rest is just sitting here. If you find anything that you can't figure out what to do with, just come get me and I'll tell you whether to keep it or not."

"Sounds good," I said. So, I got to work. I was organizing stuff and going through boxes, digging through another man's life, putting the pieces together. Golf tournament trophies and accolades, hunting gear and hidden bottles of vodka. When I came across a few specialty tools, I set them aside to ask Jennifer if I could buy them from her. When she came back after lunch, she placed a burger and a water on an old dusty kitchen table. She had to move a box of books and magazines and a stuffed mallard to make room. She told me I could keep the tools and that she didn't want any money for them.

She pointed up to a loft above the refrigerator and said that it needed to be gone through as well. I was okay with it. I saw it all as stimulus. Work is stimulus. It keeps me wired and aware and loose. I worked mostly in solitude through the afternoon. Jennifer brought back the occasional regular to introduce me to. They were puzzled by someone like me turning up at a place like this. They must have taken it as a sign that the authenticity of the place, the exclusivity, the Texan-ness of the Store was getting diluted with Missourians. At least my sister Marla hadn't found the place. However, Missourians aren't the real enemy of the Texan, a lot of the cattlemen I'd met had done business in Missouri at one time or another and liked it, and all that had been there asked me the same question about St. Louis. They all asked if I'd been across the river to the east side. East St. Louis was actually in Illinois. It was once a thriving community along the Mississippi where blue-collar jobs grew on sweetgum trees and living was safe and easy. Now it is gutted and poor. Across the river from affluent neighborhoods in St. Louis proper, it sulks. To visitors, East St. Louis is known for a handful of cheap strip clubs. This is what the Texans remembered most. They'd elbow me and nod. Their cowboy hats must have looked strange in that ghetto, if they had the courage to wear them. No, the real enemy of the Texan is not the Missourian, or the Illinoisan, but the Californian, for reasons that I don't know well enough to explain but have something to do with immigration and the fact that they're "all pussy liberals."

Around five in the evening, Jennifer told me to call it quits. As we walked out, she told me about some of the regulars. Which ones to avoid, which ones to remember.

"I'll keep the back door unlocked in case you need to use the restroom in the middle of the night," she said.

"Thanks," I said. "I noticed a few kayaks across the street. Those are your rentals, right?"

"That's right. That old building used to be a car dealership. Back then, the cars probably sold for the price of one of them stupid kayaks."

"It looks like they're the only thing holding up the ceiling," I said.

"That's my next job for you when you finish with that loft. Fix the kayak barn."

"Ok, I'll do it. I like it here. I know we haven't talked about pay yet, but what if, instead of cash today, I took one of those boats? I always wanted one, and I think it might help me see this river."

"Don't you think you'd be better off with some money in your pocket?" she asked. "You gotta feed that dog and you ain't catching no perch."

"Probably better off with money. But more bored."

"How about this, I'll pay you for today, and you can use any of those kayaks as long as you're here? When you leave town, maybe I'll let you buy one."

"Deal," I said.

CHAPTER 7 ...

Home's Guilt

The next morning, I figured I'd call my sister back. I drove the eighteen miles into Llano to get cellphone service and had breakfast at The Hungry Hunter around sunup. I called her from the parking lot while I smoked and shook the cold out of my legs.

"Marla?"

"Luke," she said. Her voice was impatient, not unsisterly though.

"Where are you?"

"Texas."

"Where at?" I didn't want to give too many details. It's easier that way. It's never easy.

"Somewhere in the middle. Middle-south. Doesn't matter," I said.

"Someone should know where you are when you do this," she said. "It doesn't have to be me, but someone in your life, someone that cares about you needs to know where you are. It doesn't help that you never answer."

"How's Dad?"

"He's hurting. It'd be nice to have help. He's wearing me out. I might have to hire a live-in nurse."

"You're the tough one. You don't need help," I meant the comment as a compliment. Or maybe a joke. I couldn't tell. Neither of us could tell what I meant.

"Not sure how long that's going to last. He screams in the middle of the night. At the pain. Sometimes at you."

"I think I can hear him," I said.

"You've been getting stuff in the mail here. Looks like it's from the state. Your lawyer says she can't get ahold of you, either. Why don't you call her back? She helped you. If anyone deserves a call it's her."

"I don't understand why she still needs to talk to me. It's all over. The case is over. I was exonerated."

"I don't know. Paperwork, I guess. Just call her," she said. Neither of us said anything for a moment, then I spoke up.

"It's been a year and I still can't sleep," I said. My face started to sweat and I kicked a rock in the parking lot.

"Yeah?" she said.

"I have these living dreams. I'll be sitting in a diner, and my booth will start swinging around the room like a carnival ride. I'm swinging past families, old men reading the newspaper. No one looks up from their plate, and I'm whizzing around the restaurant right past them. Then, the waitress comes to fill up my coffee and I realize I hadn't blinked in five minutes, and my food's cold."

"You can't sleep because you're anxious. I don't know why you're so anxious," she said. "You were found innocent. You were let go because you were innocent."

"I was exonerated because the prosecutor made a mistake. It was a technicality. If we couldn't have afforded that lawyer, I'd be in prison."

"They were trying to make an example out of you and they couldn't. You were looking at your phone, you weren't drunk, you weren't high, you were driving your dad to work, and you looked down at your phone. Everyone does it. You're not a criminal," she said. "It was just a freak tragedy. You're not a criminal." We both sat a thousand miles away from one another, pressing our phones against our temples. She started talking again. "Running from us isn't going to solve what's going on in your head, Luke. You have to turn into it, not away," she said.

"I hurt people. That woman, Anette May. She had a name. She was a nurse. I ruined her life. I see her in my dreams all bloody and half dead, the way she was that night. Do you know she was a dancer in college? The only black woman on the SLU Dance team when she was there. There was an article about her in the Post-Dispatch."

"You're not supposed to read the press. That's one thing the lawyer said not to do."

"I took away her legs. Dad's on enough opiates to kill a horse. I don't have to watch the news to see that. No. I hurt him, I hurt her. Fuck this. I have to go, Marla."

"Are you going to call your lawyer?"

"Yes."

"You have her number?"

"Yes. Thank you.

"Ok. Bye."

I hung up and started the drive back to Castell. I knew Jennifer opened at nine and I wouldn't be much later than that.

CHAPTER 8 …

A Little Reading to Do

"Hey, Doodah," she said, when I walked in.

"What's that?"

"What's what?"

"Doodah."

"You ain't never heard Doodah?"

"No," I said, as I sat down at the counter, my eyes shifting under the low brim of my hat.

"The nursery rhyme, *all the doodah day…*"

"I've heard that. Yeah," I said.

'Hey you with the broken nose singing doodah diggi doodah/ Hey you in the mighty boots singing doodah diggi doodah," she sang. "You got the nose and the boots. You're Doodah."

I'd forgotten about my busted nose. I tended to avoid mirrors.

"You're a nicknamer?" I asked.

"I am," she said.

"I don't use nicknames," I said. "I can never remember to use them in the moment. I'll come up with a good one, but when the time comes to get someone's attention I'll just say *hey* or just start talking in their direction. I'm distracted, I guess," I said.

"If you have to try to remember it, it isn't a good nickname. People like nicknames. It worked for George W.," she said.

"Really?"

"Hell yeah, he nicknamed everybody. His staffers, the press, foreign leaders. It's why everybody wanted to have a beer with W."

"I was in kindergarten when he was elected," I said.

"Well, there's your problem," she said.

Alone in the back room, I leaned a shaky extension ladder up against the square silver refrigerator and climbed into the dusty loft. The light was all below me, so, even in the daytime, the space had the dim obscurity of an attic. It felt private. In high places, you can perch and watch for danger. There's a secretiveness and thrill to being tucked away above everything else. You're enlivened. It's why kids have to pee the minute they settle into a hiding spot.

I stepped off the ladder and into the clutter, tripping. The first thing I noticed was a cardboard box with the word "Houston" written on it. Leaned against the box was a painting of a whitetail deer in an alert pose standing in a stream. I stepped over a coiled garden hose, past the painting and between two stacks of kitchen chairs with vinyl cushions and got my foot tangled in the cord of an oscillating fan. I drug it halfway across the floor hopping on one foot. I reached down to unwrap it and stumbled into a neon sign that was lying on top of a washing machine. I caught it before it crashed onto the ground and looked at it as I stood up. All it said was TITTIES in pink letters. I set it on a poker table, and when I looked up, my shoulders shot up past my ears.

"Fuck you," I said in the sideways light. For a moment, I was petrified. Turned to stone. In front of me was a bull. His two horns hooked forward, aimed right at my chest and his thick red neck was stiffened with intent. The shock punched a hole through my body. The bull was mounted at the shoulders but even with most of his body gone and eaten, he was imposing. He'd been slain, but he still held something over me. His marble eye was glassy and dead and unafraid. With a shaking hand, I reached out and plucked a red poker chip from between his lips.

I held it around its edge and wiped the dust off it with my thumb. Painted in the middle of the chip was the head of another bull with the same attitude; dead and wishing he wasn't. I held the chip close to my face. It felt half an ounce heavy and, in a way, more magisterial. Like a totem, it emanated something from the past. It felt serious and alive.

I heard a "humphhh," snort from the red bull's nose and felt warm wet steam blow across my hands and wrists. Then a thin mechanical recording of an old familiar song began from somewhere across the loft:

> *Here's a little song I wrote*
> *You might want to sing it note for note*
> *Don't worry...*

There were clothes hanging from a curtain rod that stretched between a chifforobe and an old washing machine. A wall of old dresses, men's blazers and slacks hid the far corner of the loft. I walked over. The song continued, gradually getting louder. The clothes were dusty and square and old-fashioned. I slid them to the side and ducked between two blouses and found myself standing in a little open space in the boxes and furniture, almost like the junk had been eroded and a cave was formed. The nook was surrounded on all sides with Randy's belongings. Sitting in the middle of the little cave was a roll-top desk, and in front of it was a wobbly chair that had a leather seat with stuffing spilling out of busted seams. The chair was cocked to the side as if someone had just stood up from it and planned to return. I sat down.

On top of the closed desk sat a stuffed rooster. The bird was red but covered in a thin layer of silver dust. It was locked in a dominant pose, proud, with its chest out and eyes wide. Mounted between its legs was a robotic fish, a Big Mouth Billy Bass whistling and singing *Don't worry. Be happy, now.* I recognized the toy from my childhood. It was a novelty gift popular in the early 2000s. We bought one for my grandpa for Father's Day when I was a kid. I tapped the red button and the music stopped. There was a brass nameplate under the inanimate fish that said Big Mouth Billy Bass. Under that was another wooden slab with another nameplate. This one read COCKAROO.

I lifted the tambour doors of the roll-top desk and the wooden shutters clapped lightly as I revealed their secret. Inside was a typewriter with a sheet of white paper stopped somewhere mid-sentence, still ensnared in the paper bail. Next to the typewriter was a little cardboard banker's box with papers stacked neatly inside. I lifted the first sheet of paper from the stack. All that was typed across it was:

> Go, Cockaroo!
> By
> Randy Leifeste

He'd written a book, or at least made an attempt to. It seemed as though he didn't get to finish. I grabbed the next page from the top of the pile and started reading.

CHAPTER 9 ...
A Stroke of Good Fortune

I sit and write these pages at night in the loft of the storage room of the Castell General Store, in Castell, Texas -- my first and last home. I am someone who started off with nothing and has had everything. I am not absolutely wealthy like the people I know, but I've been rich. I've worked for three men in my life: my father, who was a tight hardworking German, Henry Buttery at Buttery Company in Llano during summers in college, and Howard Clack at The Superior Oil Company. I was a marketer, a bull salesman. So, it would be against my nature if this retelling of my life wasn't, in some way, a sale. Now, some sales are stretches and sometimes you don't get exactly what you set out for, but I am going to do my best to tell you every good goddamn thing I can remember. Men my age, men reaching the end of a long ride, understand how much a body's time is worth, so, I won't waste your time on nothing that ain't either entertaining or worth your effort to know. I have spent most of my professional life showing hard-to-please men a hell of a good time, whether for their benefit or my own. I know the value of entertainment. Old age and humility has satisfied the never-fading belief in my heart that if you are nice to people, nice things happen.

No, these pages aren't just meant to drink up all your time, but meant to leave a streak of myself somewhere on this dusty earth and I hope it to be an accurate one. This volume, which is a memoir of the stories I've remembered and misremembered, repeated and stretched over the decades is, in some ways, a true registration of this cattleman's life. It's up to me to come clean. If it's worth it to you (and it might be for some in this audience) to contest me on the stories that lie in these pages I invite you to come find me. I'll be right here at the Castell General Store and we'll jaw it out over a steak. I wouldn't have sat down and written this story if I didn't believe that my family and friends will find some hearty advice in it. And, hearty advice, if it rings inside you as serviceable and bona fide, sticks to your bones like mud and can't be ignored.

It would be neglectful of me, at this point, not to mention a private motive behind this book. A stroke on the Fort Brown Memorial Golf Course in Brownsville, Texas in 1983 left me with a memory loss syndrome at the age of thirty-eight. Holes were poked in the story of my life leading up to that day. Most importantly, I cannot remember the six-month period prior to the stroke. And, this was a crucial time.

Before the stroke, I told my best friend Jaimie Jones that I'd hidden money from my wife. I smelled a divorce coming, and I knew I had to secure as much of my money as I could or she'd fight for it in court. So, I buried it. Hundreds of thousands of dollars in coffee cans and trash bags all over the family ranch in Castell. Upon waking up in the hospital, I had no idea that I'd done this until Jaimie warned me that I might be missing some money. And he was right.

Jaimie said that I never told him exactly where I buried the cash, except for that it was on the ranch. This book is my last attempt at remembering where I buried the money. Maybe writing the story of my life will help reconcile the lost episodes. I will try to detect what is real and melt away the rest. I hope that if I think patiently enough, something new will pop up. Even without the buried money, I will die a happy man, but it feels reckless not to try and recover it.

...

The Store is a party that I throw every weekend with the prettiest co-hostess in a Texas. Jennifer. When I left Castell in the late 60s, it was just a wide spot in the road. No one was here. No one came here for anything. And when I returned for good after the stroke, I had enjoyed a successful career in the cattle industry, and in politics. The spot in the road was even wider and deader, but I had money to find. I opened the Store pretty much just to keep from getting bored.

Nowadays, with the Store growing the way it has over the last decade, Castell gets all types of big-time people coming through the doors, and when they do, they're just a nobody like everyone else. They're looking for a good time.

There's a certain type of person I look out for at the Store, out-of-towners, especially ones taking pictures. We get more and more of them every year. People coming in from Austin and Fredericksburg that want to photograph the river and the old barn across the street. They take pictures of the blue bonnets along the highways.

A few years back, there was a group of guys that walked in, young guys, not ranchers or locals. They were picture-taker types. I sat down at their table and struck up a conversation. I asked them how in the hell they found Castell. I asked something about their camera and told them where they could go to find some real scenic spots to take pictures of the Llano. I told them about the trout, and about the old Count of Castell back in the Fatherland.

I said, "Hey, have y'all ever seen a 1945 Kodak Brownie?" A Brownie is an old box camera. Real sturdy and American-built. These guys were serious about pictures and they knew exactly what I was talking about. I told them I had a Brownie and that I don't show it to everyone, but, since I thought that they were sharp guys, I'd let them see it.

We were standing outside under the big live oak, "Line up against that wall," I said. "I'll take your picture." I made them close their eyes and wait a minute. They started getting excited, and started whispering to each other because they knew what they were about to see was rare. "Ok, smile, boys. '45 Brownie."

When they opened their eyes, I had pulled my pants down around my knees and bent over with my asshole wide-open, pointing at them.

...

When some rich corporate guy from Austin or San Antonio decides it's time to take his fortune and retire on some nice plot of land, the first line of business is convincing the wife. He'll take her out on a Sunday and cruise the backroads of the Texas hill country and tell her about his vision. A few hundred acres on the river where they can run cattle. They can build new or renovate an old ranch house. They can have parties. Bring the grandkids out.

By the time the road pulls them around the corner into Castell, the wife is hungry and warming up to the idea. She's in love with the land.

A local writer and friend, C.C. Bronson, gives me a copy of every book he writes and signs it: "To Randy - the most well-read man in Texas." My mother was a librarian, so, education was a important in my family. I'm the kind of guy who appreciates history. People come into the store and I show them all types of historical artifacts. Most of them are sitting in the barstools. C.C. isn't just flattering me when he gives me a copy of his latest book and signs it with that complement, he does it because he wants them to sell and he knows that no one in the hill country talks to more people in a given week than I do. I was big in the cattle business, I was big in the oil business, I played a lot of golf and I was in politics. You meet a lot of people in politics. For the last part of my life, it's been real estate and running the Castell General Store with the help of Jennifer. The real estate business and the Store accompany one another so easily and brilliantly that you'd think I planned it.

During the springtime, the Store is flooded with suburban couples just like the one I described above. In March and April, the bar looks like a draw in a rise. Folks will order a steak at the pit and a beer inside and find a seat at a picnic table under the live oak. They'll talk and admire the style of the place. A shithole, pretty much unburdened by time. I'll belly up to their table and ask them how in the hell they found Castell. Nine times out of ten, I know someone they know. The men are enthusiastic and happy to meet a local, especially one that knows the land and the families that own it. A lot of these men grew up in the suburbs, where rural living is romanticized and land ownership is the point. They drive sixty-thousand-dollar pickup trucks without a dent or scratch on them and get away on weekends to ride trails and shoot guns. They've made their money, fed their kids and decorated their wives by shaking soft hands with other soft-handed men in air-conditioned corridors and beer halls where they've idealized the working man and the dirty underbelly lives of the descendants of farmers. They'll get their steak and realize that it tastes better than any plate they've ever overpaid for in the city.

There's been a lot of poor millionaires along this river and there's cash to be made selling your daddy's farm. As the years go by, family ranches get split up because of quarrels amongst the younger generations. The inheritors. Some can't afford to keep the property because of the taxes they have to pay. So, when thousand-acre ranches get subdivided because one sibling sells out, the cowboy executives from Austin and San Antonio are sitting back at the office thrilled to hear my voice on the other end of the line telling them I've found a great deal on a couple hundred acres on the Llano River. But, there's still the wives to convince. I'll tell them on the horn to come back out to Castell to see the property, but first, a burger at the Store. Once they're here, I'll chat them up, work on them for a little bit. A little small talk, mostly aimed at the wives. For the most part, these women are educated, opinionated, rich and bored. They're readers. I can pick up that someone is a reader from a mile away and nothing makes you look more trustworthy to one of these women, than recommending a book. "Have you read C.C. Bronson's new one about George W.?" …if she looks conservative…Or, "You should pick up a copy of this book about the Texas City fire,"…if I can tell she can handle something a little more tragic. Yeah, it's all a sale.

…

One of the reasons I'm writing these stories, like I said, is to retrace my steps and find my buried money. Therefore, I ought to start with the stroke. That way, maybe you can understand just how peculiar and powerful its hold on me was. That day, funny things happened all around me and I couldn't tell the real from the imaginary. The strangest part of it all is that, although the six months prior are all gone, I can remember that morning as clear as a picture. I can recall exactly how it felt to go down, stuck inside my bubbling mind.

That morning, April 19, 1983, I pulled into the parking lot of the Fort Brown Memorial Golf Course in Brownsville, Texas right on the Mexican border. The morning was hot and bright. In a good mood and ready to win a tournament, I felt I was in my prime. I bounced out of the driver's seat with a spring in my step, went around the back of the truck and swung my golf bag out of the bed and up onto my shoulder. I wheeled around and strutted over toward the clubhouse, found a cast iron bench at the edge of the parking lot, slid the bag off my shoulder and sat down. I unzipped the high pocket and pulled out an egg sandwich wrapped in aluminum foil. Reaching into a lower pocket, I grabbed a brown paper bag and unrolled it across my knee. I pinched around in the crumpled paper bag and collected up a few slivers of deer sausage. A black coupe pulled in front of me in the parking lot and a tall polished man stepped out. Three caddies ran out of the pro shop and rushed up to him, blowing past me on the bench. Their tennis shoes clapped on the asphalt when they stopped to meet him at the driver's side door. One porter took the man's keys. The other two escorted him around the car toward the curb, one carrying his golf bag, the other holding his nuts. I exposed the innards of the sandwich and dropped a couple slices of deer sausage onto the hard egg. I took a big ole bite and looked up at the man.

"Hit 'em straight, Senator," I said. The tall politician grinned. The caddies sweated.

I finished my sandwich and washed it down with a swig of orange juice and tequila from a canteen. I wiped my mouth with the paper bag, packed myself up and walked around the corner of the white stone building to a folding table just outside the men's locker room door. A wiry old man with white hair and a pastel colored polo sat with his bony knees tucked under the tablecloth. Everything was dewy and crisp that early in the morning.

"Mr. Leifeste, how are you this morning?"

"Hey, big boy. If I was any better it would be illegal," I said. Though my marriage was falling apart, I was making money. A lot of money, so life was good.

"That's good to hear," the attendant said to me and smiled. Without looking at the paper, he ran his finger down a long list of names that sat in front of him on a clipboard. "Where are you Mr. Leifeste?" he said, holding a smile, staring right at me. He flipped the page, drug his dry fingertip down that list, then flipped back to the first page, tapped around, up and down, left and right on the clipboard. He even ran his finger off the paper and poked around on the blank tablecloth a little bit, still smiling up at me. I blinked. "Ah, there we go. Randy Leifeste. You'll be playing with Mr. Holub and Mr. Overstreet today. We'll see you on the tee box at 7:33 this a.m." I looked down at the old man's finger and read the paper upside-down.

He was right. "Looks like you'll have a little time to put your spikes on, hit some practice balls and grab a bite." Slowly, without breaking eye contact with the old man, I leaned down and picked up my golf bag and made a slow step around the table toward the clubhouse. I told him thanks.

In the locker room, I sat in a low pew and ran my hands up my face and back through my rough hair. No one was around. I folded my arms and leaned back, stretched my legs out in front of me and bounced the heels of my Justins on the tile floor.

I got up and strode over to the sink, whistling through my teeth. On the vanity sat aftershave, deodorant, and black combs in a jar of blue Barbicide, standing at attention, holding their breath. That wasn't all, either. There was hair tonic, leave-in conditioner, razor blades, shaving cream, talcum powder, foot powder, a tub of pomade. There was anything an enlightened man might need to keep smelling enlightened.

I fiddled with the bottle of aftershave, and saluted the combs. I picked up the shaving cream, sprayed some into my palm and spread a thin swath of it across the counter. With my finger, I traced a few words into the white foam, *Ya gotta want it*. I looked at myself in the mirror. With my hand and a wet paper towel, I wiped the counter half-clean, threw the rag on the floor and walked out to hit a bucket of balls.

On the practice tee, I shimmied my hips and settled into my stance. I had a wicked wide golf swing that unwound from the top like a lasso around the head of a cowboy. They were flying straight and long like always, so I made my way back past the clubhouse and toward the first hole with my bag on my back.

One of the golfer wives had set up a little table near the tee box of the first hole and was handing out cookies and refreshments. I swiped a cookie off the table, put it on my thumb and flipped it high in the air like a coin. I reached up and caught it and slammed it down on the table.

"Heads or tails?" I asked. The housewife giggled. I lifted my hand. The cookie had split into two. "Here, take heads." I handed her half and ate the other in one bite. "These cookies are so good they should be goddamned illegal, ma'am," I said and gave her a wink.

"One a day keeps the doctor away," she said.

"What does it do to lawyers?"

"Can't help you there, cowboy," she said.

On the first tee box, I met with the men that I'd be paired with. Jim Holub was a fat happy gentleman whose sister had gone to Texas A&M with me. I'd once peeled her face off a sticky fraternity house bathroom floor and returned her rightfully to her drunk friends. I wasn't into taking advantage of girls that can't even keep their eyes open. The other golfer was Terry Overstreet. He was a short athletic figurine of a man who had survived the war and wanted to golf. He took no shit or practice swings, and his only discernable defect, besides his height, was his entire face. His eyes were small and black and real far apart on his head. His lips were always pursed and they casted a shadow on his chin. His nose was pulled out two or three inches from his face and hooked downward. Somehow that nose made it through Korea without catching shrapnel or getting snagged in barbed wire. I shook hands with both men.

"Morning, Jim. Morning, Eisenhower."

On the first tee box, the head official began reciting his opening speech.

"Gentlemen, welcome to the 1983 Booger Morris Amateur Spring Championship at Fort Brown Memorial Golf Course. We'll be playing eighteen today, starting from tee number one. For notes on the playing surface: this morning, a mole tunnel was discovered on the seventeenth green. We will play through. If an unlucky shot results in a ball at rest behind the mound, and requires a player to putt over the hump, all strokes shall be marked and counted as they would in normal match play. It is not ground under repair. Also, hole number 14, as you may know, is atop a large hill that slopes down to the right of the fairway. At the bottom of that hill is the Rio Grande River. Now, there's a lot of room down there, so, if you send one down the hill, don't give up on it. However, you will have a tough look in. And, if a ball is misplayed over the river and into Mexico, it will be the player's responsibility to contact the Federales, notify them of mislaid property, and engineer its retrieval. If it were me, I'd leave it. You're out-of-bounds anyways. And as always, no biting or hitting below the belt. I'm looking at you, Mr. Overstreet." We stood with our sunburned arms crossed, listening. Hearing a man speak from a clipboard started to make me sick and a little paranoid. The official wrapped up his speech and we exchanged scorecards. "Mr. Holub will tee off first, followed by Mr. Overstreet, and lastly, Mr. Leifeste."

The fat golfer folded at the waist and put his ball on the tee. We stood behind and watched. The first hole was a downhill par four, straight ahead and honest. Mr. Holub put his drive mostly in the middle. Up next was Mr. Overstreet whose swing had a funky hitch. He held his club still and erect at the top of his backswing, then collapsed his front knee before his hands came down after and made up time. His ball was just as straight as Mr. Holub's, but he outdrove the bigger man by ten yards. On his walk back to his bag, Mr. Overstreet rubbed a scuff off of the head of his driver.

"I only brought one ball today, gentlemen," the old soldier said without looking up.

"You're going to need it," I said. I walked up, teed my ball and outdrove both men by enough to make them shake their heads. We started our walk down the swath of low-cut Wilman Lovegrass. After two well placed approach shots, me and Mr. Overstreet were on, looking in for birdie, waiting for Mr. Holub to shuffle up to his ball that he left short of the green. I reached in my pocket, pulled out my poker chip, marked my ball and picked it up. The chip was red and white with the head of a

Santa Gertrudis bull in the middle. Jaimie had given it to me after a trip to Vegas where he'd cleaned 'em out.

Mr. Holub chipped his third shot close to the pin, so it was Mr. Overstreet's turn. Mr. Holub settled up next to me on the green, rested his crossed arms atop his stomach and breathed heavily while his putter dangled from his fingertips. His golf spikes offended the grass.

"Should be a one putt. I might save par," he said competitively through fat cheeks. He slackened his stance, crossed one foot in front of the other and rested his weight on his putter. The club dug itself three inches into the grass. Across the green, Mr. Overstreet, with his long beak and flattop haircut, bent over his ball holding a woman's putter in his hands. I tilted my head looking at him. Playing in an amateur tournament is not like playing a round with friends. There's hardly any chatter. The only conversation is meaningless compliments and self-damnation.

Hole two was a dogleg right, and it went similarly. Mr. Overstreet slightly outperforming Mr. Holub, and me beating them both. Hole three was a par five with a tight fairway. Mr. Holub putted and chipped well, but continued to drive the ball weakly, while Mr. Overstreet refused to let a fat man beat him. On his third shot, Mr. Overstreet hit a soft fade up and around a live oak tree to land on the green. "Cute shot, Terry," I said. I dug around in my bag for the canteen and took a swig.

On the tee box of the sixth hole, all three golf bags sat in a row. Mr. Holub had a head cover on his driver; a hand-knit gift from his daughter in the shape of a frog's head. The wool frog sort of stared dumbly into the clouds with one crooked eye and a confused look sewn onto its face. I had spent most of the morning avoiding the head cover, never looking directly at it. But, when I approached my bag, which sat between the others, and drew my driver from its sleeve, I caught the frog's crooked eye glance over at me and wink, then snap back into line. I spun quickly away from the bags, grabbed a tee out of my pocket, marched to the tee markers and stuck it in the grass. I balanced my ball on the tee and stood erect. I took an extra breath before wiggling my hips but, as soon as I started my pre-swing ritual, the ball fell off the tee and rolled a few inches backwards.

"Dammit," I said and looked at Mr. Holub and Mr. Overstreet out of the corner of my eye with my club extended out below me.

"It's fine, partner. Take your time. No penalty for a ball falling off a tee," Mr. Holub said. I reset the ball and stepped away from it. With my chest out, I tilted my head back, swallowed and approached my stance. Right down central, and long. The two men sighed in their sweaty collared shirts. So went the next three holes, more or less, while the sun soundlessly asserted itself onto our backs and we grew victims of the dessert more and more.

At the turn, Mr. Holub waddled up to the clubhouse window and requested a golf cart and a hotlink. By rule, me, and any other player in the tournament, would have been allowed to use a cart as well if we'd asked the officials, but I like most serious golfers preferred to walk. Mr. Overstreet, not willing to compete at any disadvantage, took Mr. Holub up on his offer to ride along in the passenger seat for the back nine. Even though they drove to their balls for the rest of the afternoon, the two of them never had to wait on me. I walked quickly, and since my shots were almost always closest to the pin, I had time to get to my ball while they played theirs.

The thirteenth hole was an uphill par three. On my way to the tee marker, I walked past the frog that sat in the back of the parked cart. My nerves were starting to fry, but my game hadn't suffered, yet. In the tee box, I lifted my 7-iron high over my head then yanked it down onto the ball sending it hot and straight. It landed seven feet from the pin and rolled closer. I waited for the other two men to take their shots, and while they loaded up, I began my walk up the hill to the hole. On the green, I marked my shot with the poker chip before swiping my ball up from the grass. When I stood, I saw the cart winding up the path on its way toward me. Mr. Overstreet's ball was on the green but about 45 feet from the hole. He was up first. He hammered his putt over two long sloping ridges. The ball drew a wide curve to the left and dropped right into the hole.

"Great shot, Colonel," Mr. Holub said, as he looked at Mr. Overstreet, then to me, but I didn't say anything. I hadn't even seen the shot. I was staring suspiciously at Mr. Holub's head cover in the back of the golf cart parked at the edge of the green.

Mr. Holub addressed his ball. He had a long putt, too, about 15 feet downhill. He squared up and blew it past the hole. The ball eventually settled 8 or 10 feet below the pin. He sighed and walked around to line up another shot. This time though, he dug up some confidence and sank it.

"I'm looking like Dr. Jekyll and Mr. Dumbass," he said. I still wasn't paying attention. The sun was hard on my shoulders. "It's your shot, Leifeste," Mr. Holub said to me.

I walked over to my marker. When I bent down to pick it up, the bands of white and red that decorated the circumference of the poker chip started moving clockwise around its edge. Red after white. The bull stared straight ahead without blinking. Neon green grass behind the spinning chip dimmed and brightened as a cloud passed overhead. I stood up and blood thumped in my head. I held the marker up vertically between my thumb and forefinger and stared at it bent-necked. The red squares orbiting the bull began globing and piling up against my thumb. With nowhere to go, they started to spill off the poker chip and run down the back of my hand like blood. I put the chip in my pocket and blinked hard as I stepped up and addressed the putt. I focused on stiffening and loosening different parts of my body as I'd learned to do years ago. I fixed my arms stiff and let my chest above my diaphragm swing loosely and freely like it was on a greased hinge. To be sure my feet weren't melted into the ground I lifted them both silently, left foot first, then right, a half inch off the Bermuda grass. I drew back and sank the putt.

The entire fourteenth hole of the Fort Brown Memorial Golf Course is on the top of a ridge. Like the official mentioned at the beginning of the round, there is a steep drop to the right of the fairway where, at the bottom of a gully, the Rio Grande riverbed marks out-of-bounds. Mr. Holub and Mr. Overstreet beat me to the tee box so they hit without me.

"Took too long, son," Mr. Holub said. "I already shot."

I tried to hide the fact that I was panting and sweating heavily.

"Oh, go on ahead," I said, and swallowed some spit.

Mr. Overstreet was already standing over his ball, going through his habit of checks and wiggles. The wind rose heavy up the side of the ridge and started blowing something considerable. I stood behind him with my arms crossed and my bottom lip tucked sharply between my teeth. My eyes shifted from left to right. Down to the left, in the distance, sat the clubhouse at the bottom of a small valley. It was a stone compound, well designed and lucid; a white island floating in an ocean of apathetic rock and shrubs. I tried to focus my attention back on Mr. Overstreet, but when I looked back, he was gone, and in his place stood a five-foot tall rooster frozen at the top of its backswing. His club balanced at the tips of his wings, perfectly vertical. Instead of swinging, though, the rooster stepped back away from the ball and lowered the club.

"Too windy," he said in Mr. Overstreet's voice. Mr. Holub nodded in agreement. The bird placed his club at his side and rested his weight on it while we waited. The wind ripped red feathers from the hidden nooks of his body and carried them down the hill toward the Rio Grande. His tail feathers, reflective yellow and brown and as big as a tennis rackets, trembled as he turned his back to the increasing wind. Just ride it out, I thought and turned away from the wind and the green head cover in the back of the cart.

Impatient, I looked back over my shoulder down at the clubhouse in the valley again. The building that was stone white a second before, had turned an ominous flashing mix of red and blue. When I looked back, Mr. Overstreet was back in his collared shirt, and the rooster was gone. He hit his ball low and fast and down the middle of the fairway. As Mr. Overstreet walked past me, a live oak leaf blew off a nearby tree and stuck against the side of his big nose. He flicked it off. It was my shot. I approached my ball steadily and controlled, closed my eyes and took an extra beat. I dropped my front foot back and opened my stance. I drew the club back and swung down on the ball, pulling my hands in toward my bellybutton at the last second, sending it down the fairway; straight at first then fading right, right, right with the wind. It landed on the river side of the hill, out of sight.

"Where's that one been all day?" Mr. Holub said.

"Fuck," I said and swooped my driver down across the grass hitting the tee and dislodging it from the soil.

"Lotta room down there, though" Mr. Holub said. "You'll find it."

"Ya'll's shots are straight," I said. "Mind if I take the cart and go look for this one?"

They looked at each other. "Yes, I need to keep my blood moving," Mr. Overstreet said.

"Let me grab a couple of irons and we'll meet you by the green," Mr. Holub said. They both grabbed a six and seven iron out of their bags. I fell into the driver's seat of the golf cart and fumbled to put it in drive. The narrow fairway was balanced on top of the ridge, and I did my best to fight the vertigo. From behind the steering wheel I looked down the hill to the right toward the river. It was only trickling. Then I looked left toward the clubhouse. The red and blue blaze was leaving the clubhouse parking lot and started climbing up the hill toward me, lighting up every cart path in the valley like a bolt of electricity finding its way through the clouds.

"Gonna be a rough ride, cowboy!" the frog yelled from the back of the cart. I yelled back.

"Ya gotta want it!" I jerked the wheel to the right sending the cart down the steep grassy hill. I shifted into neutral and abandoned the speed control. Weeds smacked up against the bumper and ripped under the floorboard. The tires rolled over my golf ball with a tap-tap and kicked it up into the air. My eyes were straight ahead, downhill, and a black tunnel closed in around my line of vision.

The clubs clanked and crashed against one another as the cart rattled hectic down the hill. I looked behind me at the frog. He smiled and yelled at me over the noise.

"What did you do Randy!? They're sure after *you*!" A bouncing three-iron spun and whacked the frog right in the mouth. It threw its head back and laughed. A piece of red felt in the shape of a blood droplet fell from its lip and landed in the desert weeds.

The red and blue flashing lights came flying over the hill behind me. Three police cars fishtailed over the ridge, tearing tire marks in the fourteenth fairway. Mr. Overstreet was frozen at the top of his backswing when blue and red lights swerved around the two men. They looked at each other, then down the hill toward me.

"He's got my goddamn scorecard," Mr. Overstreet said from the top of the ridge. I crashed down into the shallow bed of the Rio Grande and straight into a boulder. I was knocked unconscious.

...

When I woke up in the hospital. The nurse was confused when I asked about the police. She said there were no police, only an ambulance in the parking lot of the country club, but I was too far gone to have seen those lights. I rested my head back on the pillow. Then, the doctor came in. He said that I'd had a stroke and that they needed to run a few more tests, but that most likely I was going to be fine. Before he left the room, he told me that there were two women in the lobby waiting to see me. One claimed to be my girlfriend. The other claimed to be my wife.

CHAPTER 10 ...

No One Goes to the Zoo to See the Canaries

I heard someone walk into the back room and I froze, the pages still in my hands.

"Luke?" I heard Jennifer's voice somewhere below me. I didn't respond. I couldn't see out of the little hideaway, and I knew there was no way she could see me. I heard her foot hit the bottom rung of the ladder. "Luke, you up there?" she said. I stared at Cockaroo the stuffed rooster. I'd fallen into something face first and I had to keep it a secret. There was money hidden in rusted coffee cans all over Randy's ranch like rotten Easter eggs, and the Easter Bunny was wigged out, forgetful and dead. It was there for the taking. With that money, I could stay on the road forever. I heard her at the bottom of the ladder. "Luke, you sleeping up there?" I tilted my head back and closed my eyes and pushed some drool out the corner of my mouth. Nothing happened for a moment. "You in the bathroom?" she said softly, sort of to herself. Then I heard her boots tap the concrete floor as she left the room. I sucked the drool off my chin, folded the corner of the page I'd been reading so I knew where to pick back up and threw the stack of papers back in the box.

I slid down the ladder and climbed over piles of crap to get to the garage doors. I pulled the seven-iron that was wedged in the track and slid the door up a couple feet. I rolled under it through a puddle of rain water. I closed it silently and ran to the backyard pulling off my wet shirt and slipped into the van through the sliding door. Cane lifted his head from his pillow.

"Quiet, buddy," I whispered. I was lying on the bed with my boots on and shirt off for a few seconds when I heard a thin knuckle tap on the sliding door.

"Luke, you in there?" I let her knock again before I slid it open and looked at her through squinted eyes.

"How long have I been out?" I asked.

"Well, I don't know. Last I saw you, it was like nine. I was gonna ask if you wanted lunch."

"I'm not hungry. I had a serious headache. I had to get out."

"Sleep as long as you need, Doodah."

"This is the only place I can," I said. She slid the door shut and I exhaled and laid back on the bed and stared at the ceiling with my arms stretched over my head. I reached into my pocket and pulled out the poker chip. I held it a few inches from my face, looking at the snarling bull in the middle of the ring. It didn't blink.

I lied around with the door open so the breeze could wander in, and the dog could wander out. The sun had gone down and the Store was alive with a party. I could hear it. The porch lights were on, but the small glow wasn't enough to muddle the stars. I walked around to the front and the same two men who were there smoking and talking the night I'd arrived, were there again.

"It ain't gonna rain," the man in the black hat said, loudly over the music.

"Rain?" white hat asked.

"It ain't!" black hat yelled leaning forward in his chair.

"You don't think it'll rain?

"No, sir."

"Oh, it'll rain. I'll bet you a bottle of vodka it'll rain two inches tomorrow," white hat said.

"Who?" black hat said.

"Yes'ir, two," white hat said.

"What do you wanna bet?" black hat asked.

"I'll bet a bottle of vodka on't," white hat said.

"Ok, but we're using my rain gauge," black hat said.

White hat sat back in his chair and drew a puff of his cigarette, "And, we're using my rain gauge. You'll drill a hole in yours."

I walked past them through the door. The reception was warmer this time. I had been introduced to some of the regulars. There was Mike and Sweet Linda. They lived down the road. Mike had a big red face with jet-blue eyes, and Sweet Linda had a little white face and sweet bangs. There was Chris, who Jennifer introduced me to because she thought the two builders in town should get to know each other. She liked putting people in touch like that. There was Harlan, the fly-fisherman, who, it turned out, was engaged to marry Jennifer. And, of course, there was Ickie. It didn't take long until him and I were out on the porch smoking a cigarette listening to him sermonize about zoos and the nature of man.

"There's some animals we just care about more, dude. And the rest are just there, y'know. There's some you're stoked about. I mean like the heavy hitters at the deal…at the, uh, zoo. No one goes to the zoo to see the canaries, man. Or what about the squirrels that's just runnin' wild in there? People're walking around the zoo and a squirrel runs between their legs and they don't give a fuck, man, but they'll drag their ass a half a mile to see the penguins through the hockey glass, y'know, fuck. That squirrel was just hanging out and they built up a zoo around him. And the zoo people are like, 'Hey, we can save a lot of money, don't have to build a squirrel cage.' The whole thing's a squirrel cage, man. But, he comes and goes when he please. Or, what about the ducks that land on the pond? They're just like the squirrels. People walk right past 'em. The ducks can jet whenever they want to. I bet they smuggle in cigarettes and porn fer all other guys, y'know, frickin' flyin' right over the gates, man."

He looked out over the night, wide-eyed and satisfied with his theory. He floated his open palm in front of his face while he took a drag of the cigarrette wedged deep between his black cracked fingers. "So how long you here, man?" he asked with a chest full of smoke. He blew it out.

"As long as it takes," I said. I felt like I had to talk cool when I was talking to Ickie. He dug it.

"I dig it," he said. We stood there a minute smoking. "Oh, say man, my daughter gon' be rollin' into Austin in a couple weeks. Remember I tole you she's a painter, well, turns out she got herself a van like her big brother and wants to giddy up." Parts of Ickie's face shifted to reveal its big inevitable smile.

"Is she coming here?" I asked.

"Yeah, man. Told her to come on out," he said. "Maybe ya'll can hang."

"That'd be cool." My heart jumped a little.

"Whatchu doin' two days from now? I could use some help," he said. "Randy's son needs me to get this ranch truck runnin'. Wants to sell it 'cause it's been sittin' for years on his ranch and they want the money out of it."

"His kids live around here?"

"No, they jetted to the city when he died. Meet me at Randy's house Monday morning and we'll go," he said.

"Which one is his house?" I asked.

"It's over there 'cross the river. Come off the bridge and go left and it's the first one on the gravel road. When them old Germans got here, they made Castell on the north side of the river. For some reason, the town moved over here at some point. That's a old frickin' house over there, man. Been there a lotta years. Like a hunerd," he said. "Two hunerd, maybe."

I knew this was my chance to check out Randy's ranch. I would be able to scout it out as I worked with Ickie during the day, but I knew any digging would have to be done at night. I told him that I was willing to help and that I'd see him there Monday.

When everyone left the Store that night, I stuck around to help clean up. I still had a beer and was finishing it while Jennifer and I talked.

"Why are you doing this for me?" I asked. "It seems like the locals here want to keep this place a secret," I said. "You're making me part of it."

"It's what Randy would have done. He wanted all types of people here. He wanted to show it off. The river. The flowers. It's all worth showing off. Plus, I need help. I told you that."

"You don't make Harlan stick around and help clean up?" I asked.

"No, I told him to go home. He comes out on the weekends and a couple days a week if he can," she said. "It works for us."

"Does he want you to move to the city?" I asked.

"I have a lot going on here. I can't leave. He's got his business in Austin and I wouldn't expect him to give that up. I don't want to owe anyone anything," she said. "I want to do it on my own. My second marriage, I went into business with my husband, and at first it was rewarding. We were accomplishing things together, you know. But eventually it just became a partnership. A business partnership. We lived together, ate together, worked together...Once that love left, we were just business partners that shared a closet. We lost that empathy for one another. When we were in love, I did everything for him. And I enjoyed it, but once the love melts off, and you look at it bare, it's just paperwork. I don't want to be involved in that again. I want to make something I can be proud of. Me, I," she dug her finger into her chest, "...I can be proud of, not anyone else. I don't want to take anything from anyone," she didn't look up from the floor she was sweeping. "I want to get to a point where I can give, not take. Everyone should start something on their own," she said.

"That's America, right?" I said. She ignored the question, never too interested in politics.

"I think you're looking for a home," she said. She stopped sweeping and rested her folded hands on the tip of the broom handle. "Don't you think so?"

"I have a home in St. Louis," I said.

"That's where you're from. I mean a home."

"I left because I had to. I had to see the West. It turns out I had to see the East, too. And the South. And Canada, some. People tell me I'm brave to pack up and leave it all behind and chase the dream. I don't know if I believe them. Sometimes the brave thing to do is to stay. I was terrified of staying home, so I fixed up this van, threw my tools in the back and claimed I was going to fish my way to the Pacific, but I knew that was just something to call it. An adventure. What it really was was an excuse to flee."

"You must have caused some damage back home."

"Yeah, a lot before I left. More if I'd have stayed."

"I bet they miss you," she said pulling a bag of beef jerky out of her warm back pocket. She took a piece out and held it between her teeth then rolled the bag back up, squeezing all the air out. She slid the tough plastic packaging back into her pocket. She saw me watch her. "It softens it," she said.

The next morning was Sunday and I walked across the bridge to get a closer look at Randy's ranch from the road in the daylight. Three smallies hovered in the current below the concrete, facing upstream, static but flicking their tailfins in coordination. They were so close to the surface that the morning sun found hints of yellow in their green-brown backs. I made it to the north side of the river, the side that I had fallen asleep on when I'd arrived. I walked up the red dirt road to the west, over a cattle guard with my flat human feet, and past a pasture that was so dense with tall white prickly poppy it looked like you couldn't walk through it without drawing blood. The house wasn't far down the road and when I walked up the drive, there were a couple black heifers grazing in a pin next to an old crusty red barn.

Later that night, after all the steaks and beef ribs had been sold off the pit, I snuck back into the Store to spend some more time with the book. I needed to learn as much as possible before I got my chance to go onto the property with Ickie.

CHAPTER 11 ...

Watch the Road, Randy

Most of my memories are slippery. I don't know with certainty that the pictures in my mind are even mine, or if they were put there from a lifetime of stories and dreams and vodka. But others are clear and complete like a movie playing right behind my eyes.

I was about five years old, and my daddy and I was on the dirt road in front of the house. It was around sunset. We were about a quarter-mile away from the hog pins and he let me down off his shoulders.

"Watch the road, Randy," he said. "I bet we'll see deer tonight." It was a perfect night for them to be out, too. It was a little overcast, which made for an early dusk, and there was no wind. Sure enough, we weren't walking for long and a doe and two fawns got spooked and bounced across the road, coming up from a drink at the river. "There they go, Randy," he said, pointing out at the deer. Not hearing a response, he looked down to see me shuffling along, my neck bent and my eyes looking down at my boots. I hadn't seen the deer. He told me to watch the road, and I always listened to my daddy. He laughed and patted my head. He said, "Guter Junge."

Most of my early childhood is gone — lost in the cow paths of my wrinkled mind — but another memory that's lasted took place during an afternoon in springtime Castell. I was just a tyke. My best friend Jaimie and I were both drug to a birthday party celebrating some kid we didn't know. We were standing around with two or three other nervous boys all pulling on our momma's dresses and drawing circles in the sand with our toes. I didn't know any of them, and didn't trust 'em neither. But, we all warmed up, the way kids do. Eventually, someone pulled out a cap gun and started blasting away at rabbits and birds. I fell in love with that gunpowder smell. That cap gun got everyone buzzing and playing together and gave our mothers a chance to catch up on small-town gossip. See, Castell, at the time of my birth, was on a decline, not completely empty, there was still something of a town here, and the church was still afloat and full of Methodists, but the real boom came in the twenties and thirties before I was born and before the drought. At that time, there was upwards of 200 citizens. But my whole life, Castell's been on its way dying, and now that I'm fixing to die, it's on the upswing again. Thanks to me.

    We were aiming that cap gun at stumps and birds and each other and were having a good time and eventually ran from the barn down to the river to see what else we could shoot. It didn't take long until one of the boys came up on a water moccasin swimming across the stream. It was coming to our side of the river, so we all piled over to the bank, and waited for it to get to us. As soon as it hit the sand, it bolted toward the bushes to get away. But, we had it surrounded on the beach. I ain't never met these kids before in my life but we were a good team catching snakes. Seemed that they all knew what they was doing and we could communicate with just eyes and points and screeches. The snake was all coiled up and had its cotton mouth wide open hissing at us, then it leaped at one of the boys and caught his pant leg. I had the cap gun in my hand and when the snake jumped, it scared me so bad I must have jerked the trigger because the little hammer went off. Pop! The snake stopped dead in its tracks and rolled over, belly up still hanging on the boy's pant leg. We all looked at each other like we'd just landed on the moon. I went over and picked the snake up by the tail and it was limp as a noodle. I ran up the hill to the house to show my mother. She was sitting on the porch cross-legged with a lemonade in her hand. I came up behind her with the snake, terribly proud of what I'd done, and put the prize in her lap.

That cottonmouth must've had enough of playing dead and it needed to shove off 'cause as soon as I put it in her lap, it wiggled to life and jumped down from off her leg and onto the porch. All the women screamed and some of them stood on their rocking chairs while the snake scurried across the floor. I shot the cap gun at him, but I must have missed because he found a wide crack in the porch boards and got away.

...

Years later, on a Wednesday. I was probably getting on age nine, and I was sitting in the tabernacle next to my mother in her white shoes, and daddy in a coat and tie. It was a boring place, the tabernacle. It was just a shed in a field. It had no walls, just cedar posts along the outers to hold up the tin roof. Outdoor church, it's plain to me, is just as boring as indoor church, only buggier. And, I had an affliction that, you could say, did me a disservice when it came to my rehearsing of the doctrine.

Father Mudder was groaning and preachering in the heat and the bugs, but I wasn't paying attention to any of that dragged-on mess. I reached down below my seat and scraped my fingers across the gravel, feeling through the rocks to find a stone small enough to fit into the fold of my finger, but with enough weight to cut through the air. When I did find one satisfactory, and bounced it in my hand and got to know it, I'd look around for to make sure there wasn't anyone looking. Then, I'd whizz it down the pew past Jaimie and his mom and dad and sister, past the Travis's and their one-eyed baby daughter, past ugly Ned and Yoho Fischer and their daddy, and I'd crack the post and be sitting back up in my seat before anyone heard it hit. It can feel right satisfying when you hit a cedar post square with a rock from twenty-odd feet away, and any self-respecting person knows the business of flinging rocks is a disorder that takes aholt of you before you understand what you're into, and can be addicting and detrimental to your scriptural studies, especially if you have a healthy pile of good ones under your feet. It's sticky work flipping rocks past the whole town and sitting up in your seat and listening for your reward. Even with Father Mudder up there preachering, a rock tapping a cedar post has a distinctive-type sound, a bright little tick noise, that one can pick out among the expected clack of a Wednesday morning tabernacle. It's a sound that one's mother, particularly, can become anxious of and reactive to. That Wednesday, though, I picked up a rock and spun it down the aisle the same way I always did, but Ned Fischer saw it coming. Him and his brother Yoho were always drug by their ears along the river to the tabernacle on church days against their nasty wills.

    They lived somewhere upriver, between here and Mason, but I wasn't allowed to know where exactly and didn't much care to know, neither. Their mother was gone and dead and their poor daddy thought that the church would save them, though it wasn't doing any good on them or his self. He was drunk all the time, even the mornings. Even in church. Ned was seventeen and Yoho sixteen at that time. He stuck his paw out and snatched that little pebble right down out of the air. He looked up the row at me and grinned with his yellow teeth. Then he flicked the little pink granite stone into the back of Mrs. Mudder's head. Ned and Yoho were a mean and nasty and ugly breed and it wasn't just that day I learned it. The preacher's wife whipped around and gave me a huffy look because, by then, I was known for getting' pre-occupied in church and flipping rocks. Even now I can still hear my momma's voice in my ear telling me that I've been told, and been told, and been told that I can't spend all morning throwing rocks and not listening to Father Mudder and his preacherings, and that there ain't no rocks in heaven, only clouds, and throwing rocks and throwing clouds is different because they don't fly the same so there's no use practicing and getting good at tossing rocks because I'm going to be mighty bored and embarrassed in heaven if the only thing I learn how to do on earth is shoot rocks at the back of Mrs. Mudder's head when all they got up there is clouds. But hot damn, I loved flinging rocks and I might have thought I had a decent little addiction hanging on me at the time, or at least the guilt of one. But hey, after hundreds of hours sitting in that buggy tabernacle, some church stuff did sink in. I heard Father Mudder say once that, in Eden, every kind of precious stone adorns you. You can look it up in The Bible. They got ruby, they got topaz, diamond, beryl, onyx, jasper, sapphire, turquoise, and emerald. That's a pretty good lot of rocks, half of them you ain't gotta go to Eden for neither, you can find them by setting your feet in the Llano and letting the water roll them past you.

We didn't have much, but with a daddy that's a farmer, and a mother that's the head of the town library, I had plenty of land to run around on when I wanted to be outside, and plenty of books to keep me snug when I was inside. I read and reread Tom Sawyer and Huckleberry Finn close to a dozen times each. I would often spend the entire morning reading Mark Twain, or The Hardy Boys and, in the evening, when I would get done with whatever chores my daddy had for me, I would go down to the river and reenact the scenes from the book.

I always wondered if Mark Twain believed he was any smarter or stupider than the characters he was writing. I always liked Huckleberry Finn more than Tom Sawyer. He wasn't the smartest of boys or finest or most well-behaving either, but he was real, and he had more shape to him than any real person I knew, besides maybe Jaimie.

I spent many adventures with them boys. If you get caught in a real good book, you can't decide just exactly who you are and who you aren't. The pictures are part of you. They're part of your memory, whether the memory is yours to begin with or not.

One night I was having tough luck sleeping, and woke up in the middle of the night went to get some water, but my mother, she was awake sitting at the kitchen table.

"Randy, what are you doing up this late?" she asked.

"I can't fall asleep. I need a splash of water," I said.

"Is something keeping you up?"

"Just a ghosty dream," I said.

"What was in it?" she asked with her light voice. My whole life she sounded like a singer on stage, talking in between songs.

"Oh, it seems like nothin' now. I was just reading about Huck Finn before I went to bed, and it sort of lingered. I's on the part he carves up the pig and uses the blood to 'scape his daddy," I said.

"I thought those books were supposed to be funny," she said.

"No, they are good!" I said. I was afraid she might take them away if I wasn't delicate in my interpreting. "It's just some things are brutal, but Huck explains 'em to you in a real soft way, so it keeps you from feeling too tragic. In the book, he chops up a pig, and that's what I saw in my dream, a hacked-up pig staring at me in the barn."

"I'm surprised you get worked up about a gory pig for as many hogs as are on this farm. And dead ones, too," she said.

"I ain't scared of a pig," I told her. "I was just squirrelly readin'. I didn't want Huck to get caught, I reckon."

"Dreams are of a strange design," she said. "You can't control them. Sometimes you can shake them, but sometimes you get shook."

My mother was the smart and sweet one. She had a way of understanding people and their fears and their shortfallings. My father was always louder and a little ornery, especially when it came to athletics.

I was an exceptional athlete. And my sport, if I had to pick one, was baseball, though I played basketball and football and tennis, too. In one baseball game, I hit three homeruns my first three times up to the plate, and on my last at bat I hit a double to the wall, and when the game was over, on the way home, my father asked me why the fourth one didn't go over the fence.

I could hit, and I loved stealing bases. It's the purest thing in the game, and some guys go their whole lives thinking they can't do it or shouldn't try. It's a mental contest as much as it is a physical one. You have got to recognize patterns, you have got to recognize tendencies, laziness, personality.

There was a game in Llano that I'll never forget. I was twelve years old. The pitcher came set, tucked his chin into his left shoulder and peeked towards first. One…two…stride toward the plate. Some people think you steal off first movement. If you do that, you're already late. You need to know when the pitcher's going home before he does.

It was the fourth inning and he hadn't tried to pick off much. He was strong but he was too simple to know when and why he was getting beat. I watched one more pitch to get the timing down. One…two…stride toward the plate. Too simple. Jaimie knew I was going on the third pitch. He had no strikes, so he was taking.

Hesitation in sports, like in life, will ruin you. Kill that doubt that comes just before you throw the lever and spark your muscles into action. If you are *thinking* about when to go, you might as well take your cap off, and walk right into the dugout and start untying your spikes. Good base stealers feel themselves sliding into second before they even take the first step off first. In their mind, it's an instantaneous exchange of inclination for result.

He toed the rubber. One..I took off with an involuntary twitch…two…stride toward the plate. I found myself in the middle of the desert, unsafe and panicked. I heard a young voice crack behind me.

"Runner!"

The ground moved silently below me, just a blurred patch of hot Texas soil. I'd been out there too long. It was like I didn't stride at all, just glided. I should be there by now, I thought. But I wasn't. The ball popped in the catcher's mitt and I heard a shuffle. My head was down but I could sense the second baseman moving in towards the bag. I began to slide. Don't fall over onto your hip, sit straight down and land on the fatty part of your ass. I was in underneath the second baseman, I could sense it. The throw must have been high and to the right, because he jumped toward me and over me. All I saw was the bottom of his spikes. My head snapped back from the blow, and in a flash, the pale blue sky was the only thing holding me. Then it went black.

That was the first time in my life I'd ever been knocked out. Awake. Then nothing. That's how I imagine death. Do you remember what it was like before you were born? Of course, you don't. There's nothing, then there's everything. Death is just the same in reverse.

...

My life, at the time, was all about sports and bumming with Jaimie. It was baseball in the spring and summer, but winter meant basketball.

I was done dressing out and was picking at the paint chipping off the bench not paying much attention to anything. Lead paint probably. When we were in junior high we practiced in the high school gymnasium on nights that the varsity and junior varsity were off. There were about eight kids in the locker room and I was sitting next to a guy named Clyde Yesper. Clyde had leg hair before the rest of us and pimples, too. He was the tallest and slowest and clumsiest kid on the team. He had this crackling voice that he fought to control like a bucking bronc.

"Ya'll gotta 'lectric icebox in yo' house?" he asked me. "It's an icebox, only it don't use ice, it runs off 'lectric power." He didn't wait for a response. "We just got one. Yup, we are electrified. The fella from the power comp'ny gave us an icebox for free if only we let his men hang 'lectric wires across our farm.

They ain't dangerous or nothing, they just dangle there," he was trying to take off a boot that was stuck to his foot. "So, my daddy said sure you can run them wires on our farm and into our house. My daddy was mighty excited about it. Said he felt modern. The modernist thing we ever done. Momma said that daddy needed something good like this to happen to him ever since he got his foot stomped by a steer. Thought they's gonna have to chop't off, but it's healing O.K. wrapped on the board. Boy, he was depressed about that foot, one night my brother said something that hounded 'im, and he got aholt of Merl and threw him acrost the kitchen table bouncin' on one foot the whole time. But, since now we got that 'lectric icebox, twice a day he props that mangled foot up there and cools't off. And the cool must make it all the way to his head, because he ain't never throwed none of us since he got cool feet. He says it relieves the itchin' and the engorgin'," Clyde looked up from his boot and I nodded when he caught my eye. He continued, "Our land is right square in the middle of the county, so it was in a spot real adv'ntageous to the power comp'ny for their natwork. The power man said he dreamt of wires that crist-cross the whole state of Texas and that he had a vision for every ranch home in the county to be hot by the end of the decade. And by hot, I mean cold, 'cause they gon give e'rbody a band new icebox when they get set up. We got one, at least. Boy, I slept goo-oood last night. Put my pillow and blanket in the 'frigerator and kept it chilly until I turnt in. Now my little brother Merl and sisters put they linens in there and crowd't up 'cause they saw it was such a good idea. My daddy and my momma put they's in there, too. We started taking the food out to make room for the pillows and sheets and my brother even start putting his socks in there to help with the smell and I think it's a fine idea. Here, smell this one." He put a sock in front of my face. By this point he had gotten both his boots off, and hadn't been wearing socks underneath them. The sock he had in his hand was a separate sock that he had been carrying around in his pocket.

"No, I'm not going to do that, Clyde," I said. I looked up at Jaimie. He was laughing so hard his face was contorted and red behind the wadded up jersey he held over his nose and mouth.

"Well, it stinks. But Merl's? His don't. He gets 'em near frozen every night. Knocks the smell right off 'em."

My house had had power for most my life. We were one of the first houses in the area to get electricity since we lived along the river, and the road followed the river, and the powerlines followed the road. I didn't tell Clyde though.

"I gotta get going, Clyde. I'm on lights tonight," I said. Jaimie was still leaning with his back against the wall of lockers wiping the tears out of his eyes.

The gymnasium was a place where commotion was necessary, so when it was without noise, and unlit and empty, you realized that it was only steel beams and concrete and orange-colored paint that kept the roof up. I stood in the corner a minute, with my hand on the switch, and let the emptiness roll across the three hundred feet of hardwood floor and crash over me in waves that smelled like dust and polyurethane. I was eager to start high school. I couldn't know it then, but the next four years in that gym would be where I shined. Two all-district honors and one state championship.

Square moonlight came through one high window on the opposite wall. I threw the switch and the lights hummed, but the gym stayed dark and the moonlight held. Those old mercury vapor lights took about fifteen minutes to get completely bright. It's a strange feeling waiting for the lights to come on. An unremarkable development, really. You don't notice the progress, but once the room grows pale you can't remember how the darkness looked just a few seconds earlier. Slowly the absence which is huge and undeniable, begins to dissolve and the gym starts to look a little familiar. The emptiness scatters into the corners and electric light takes its place. You keep thinking that it's reached full-beam, but still it grows more and more clear.

My teammates ran in through the doorway behind me dribbling rhythmically like a platoon on march. I picked up a loose ball that was resting near the bleachers and joined the procession around the gym.

We stretched and shot around for a while until drills, then we started running plays. I was the point guard. The first play we practiced was simple. The goal was to get the ball to Clyde but first Jaimie and I worked it back and forth, drawing the defense out then we'd dump it underneath. The first time we ran it Clyde couldn't get away from the defender or box him out at all, so neither Jaimie nor I had an opening to pass it in. He just stood in one place hoping from one foot on to the other, like he was standing barefoot on hot sand. He was doing a lot of moving, but he wasn't moving anywhere, if you know what I mean. Coach blew the whistle. He pulled the big kid aside and told him that the play wouldn't work if he didn't hustle to get open. So, we ran it again. And again, he just stood there with his hands above his head and his mouth open shifting his weight from one foot to the other. The defender bounced around in front of him energetically with his arms waving up and down. Coach blew the whistle again, and walked up to him, grabbed him by the arms and moved him left and right. The next time we ran it, Clyde started shuffling his feet and actually broke loose of the defender but not enough for an open pass. When I lobbed the ball into him, it got stolen. We ran it again and again, and every time, the ball would either get stolen or rattle around in his hands and up his arms and bounce off his chest and roll away. And every time, he'd chase the rolling ball into the corner or out into the hallway and bring it back to me.

"I'll get it this time," he said. "Just keep chunkin' it in to me, I'm fixin' to get it." He turned around and jogged back to the basket.

After a few more failed tries coach stopped practice again and talked to his big man. Coach was desperate to make Clyde his star. He gave him ten times the attention he would have given a smaller kid. Jaimie walked over to me and crossed his arms and we watched Coach as he grabbed Clyde's arms and feet and moved them around mimicking athletic movement.

"He's got hands like feet," Jaimie said to me. "We need to put him in the ice box." Coach had given it his best shot and walked back to half court. Jaimie grabbed the ball out of my hands and walked towards the hoop. "Here, I think I can help." Jaimie took the ball in his right hand and brought it back past his ear like a football and whizzed it as hard as he could right at Clyde's head. The big country boy caught the ball two inches in front of his face. He lowered it to his side and looked dead at Jaimie who was walking quickly toward him.

"Don't touch me, pal," Clyde said. "I don't want to get violent."

"That's what it feels like to catch a pass," Jaimie said. "I plan on winning a game in the next five years." He took the ball out of Clyde's hands, who looked confused as hell at first then he smiled.

I lined everyone up again. Coach blew the whistle.

"Alright, let's run it one more time," he said.

I passed the ball over to Jaimie, he passed it back, Clyde moved around a little, and Jaimie sent it back to me. When I saw my opening I took the ball in one hand, reared back and threw it like a rocket right at his face. He went to protect himself and when he opened his eyes he saw that the ball was stuck between his hands.

I couldn't believe it! He'd caught it clean. Everyone in the gym stopped. They couldn't believe either. The only sound was Clyde as he made one dribble and turned to face the basket. The defense just stood there in amazement as Clyde threw the ball against the bottom of the rim. It bounced straight down, hit off his forehead and rolled out of bounds.

"Owp, dern it," he said to himself. I closed my eyes.

He jogged over towards the door to pick up the ball. It had come to a rest against the wall under the light switch. When he reached down for it, his long body looked like a broken windmill that had been bent in half in a lightning storm. He reached forward shuffling a little. His big feet couldn't keep up and he tripped. On his way down, he reached towards the wall to catch himself, and through all of his flailing, he grabbed the lever and cut the lights. No one saw him hit the ground, but the thumps and squeaks from his heavy bones hitting the wall and his rubber shoes looking for grip on the floor made a hell of a racket. The gymnasium went as black as outer space. The whole team sighed.

I'd stay over at Jaimie's house all the time as a kid. We was about fifteen. We'd laugh so hard at nothing. The kind of laughter where your stomach tightens until think you might never inhale again and you wouldn't mind if you didn't.

We did a lot of stuff to keep ourselves busy and entertained. We played a lot of baseball and basketball. I was always busy with the farm. My daddy always had something to keep me occupied if I wasn't. Or I was up at the library helping my mom. Jaimie and me hunted a lot and enjoyed it. Hunted for deer, jackrabbit, coon. Anything we could shoot, we would. I used to go coon huntin' with Jaimie for money. There was one night, we were walking the road up here. We were just walkin' and it was cold.

"Don't move," I whispered, my breath kind of tumbled white through the lamplight. I saw eyes moving in the underbrush. "Behind that mesquite. Big one," I said. Jaimie sidestepped to get up behind me and rested the fore end of the rifle on my shoulder there. I always had kind of sloped shoulders because I had a high behind-the-neck muscle. I squeezed my left eye closed, the one nearest to the gun barrel.

Jaimie pressed his warm cheek up against the cold gun and lowered his finger from off the steel and onto the trigger.

He manipulated the barrel in the moonlight, and with one eye pinched shut, nestled that far sight into the crack on the rear sight and covered the grey fur with the bead.

He said, "She sees us."

"Take your time," I said. "She ain't gonna run." Jaimie waited for my breath to melt away between the sights. He squeezed the trigger slow. That old pap shattered out across the river. The big bitch tumbled and rolled, shook and spun like an electrical wire cut to the ground. She was crashing all against the brush and against herself. Jaimie put another one in her. She shuttered one more time and came to rest in a cactus. We walked up to it. It was laying there all leaky with its fur matted down and messy with blood. Jaimie picked it up by the legs. "That's an eighteen-pound coon, boy," he said. Though, size didn't matter much. The fur trader paid the same for a coon no matter the size of it. We saw that coon right off the side of the road and figured that would be our good luck for the night. The rest we were going to have to work for.

The fur trader would come through and give you fifty cents for a coon skin, two dollars for a ring-tail. Just a couple years later though, the price shot way up and you could get a few dollars for a coon skin in Houston because the Russians were using them to make coats. You could also sell the carcass. They say the black folks would eat 'em. They'd mix the coon meat and sweet potatoes, have sweet potato coon. You'd never catch me eating no coon. And I was poor. No, the black fellas wasn't just poor they liked it. It's greasy kind of meat. Anyways, there we were with the dead raccoon and had to skin it. It shouldn't take you more than five minutes to skin a coon, and Jaimie and I were as good as anybody at doing it.

We threw the big bitch next to the sandy road to come back for later because it wasn't no use carrying eighteen pounds of coon over your shoulder and a rifle and a lamp and trying to keep quiet. We worked our way down toward the river through the thick brush making sure to step straight up and straight down so as not to kick the branches and rocks under our feet and send one down the hill to crash in the water and scare away any chance we might have of making another fifty cents. That was good money. We made a lot of money that way in those years. The moon was big and the sky was clear and cold and that was a favor since you could see better on those nights. We walked for a while with no luck. Jumped a couple deer but that was all and we weren't really looking for deer and weren't really in the mood to go through the whole messy process of shooting and cleaning and dragging one. Not that we weren't capable, just not really in the mood for the whole thing. Plus, with just a .22 you'd have to hit a deer mostly in the head or neck to really kill it right and it was dark and the blood trailing would have been too much of a chore even with carbide lamps. We walked and walked and everything seemed stiff and unwelcoming the way it does in the cold moonlight. Rocks tumbled louder against one another, branches snapped crisp off when we bumped into them. A twig caught me in the ear and I flinched. And when I did that, I thought I heard something behind me. You know how when it's real quiet and still out in the woods at night, sometimes you move unnaturally quick like that and you hear yourself move, but you're not too sure it was yourself that you heard or something else? I was more or less a small kid and a little skittish. I stopped and said something to Jaimie about what I heard but we kept on walking. The river can be loud down there. Things are moving and shifting and floating by and crashing into one another in the maelstroms. You're often not too sure what you're hearing.

    We had one of them old pump .22s. You'd pump it and it made that clean little chuck-chuck sound. You could fit something like thirteen or fifteen shells in one of those. If you went through that many you'd be sitting fat at the end of the night, and that ain't realistic. But, we carried a lot of bullets anyway because when you're a kid you always think optimistic when it comes to hunting.

Jaimie was always a bit taller than me and more into some shit, too, at least when we were young. Jaimie was carrying the thin riffle belly-up tipped back over his right shoulder with his finger always ready near the trigger and we came up on a clearing on the riverbank and saw a light real far off downstream and across the river. He says, "God damn, I'm gonna shoot that light out." And this light was a ways off, I mean like a mile off. Real little, just sort of flickering and twinkling there. So, he aimed kind of high and lets one go so the bullet could fall right into that light. He sent it screaming down the river into the cold night. Of course, nothing happened. We felt that hollow feeling you get when you fail at something that no one expects you to really do anyways. I swatted the gun down after he shot and told him don't waste any more shells, plus he was going to scare the raccoons off. I thought it was no use shooting someone's lights out. I was always the quieter of the two and had decent morals. It was because my mother was such a saint. She wasn't someone that could do any harm to anyone. She was always interested in reforming the poor and sick and dumb. That's the kind of folks she was interested in. Anyways, we started back to walking. You could walk ten miles in a night coon hunting with those carbide lamps, and go up onto anyone's property you wanted because everyone did it.

  We kept walking and creeping along all quiet and slow through the thick part of the riverbank on the sloped side really looking to come up on a coon. And that moon was doing us a big favor shining so bright that night. A big cold moon up there shinning so hard on the river we could see our shadows. It made us right optimistic. Like something was going to happen. Like there was some luck in it for the both of us, and having already killed one whopper so early in the night, we were feeling considerable upbeat even though the cold was ripping through our thin dirty jackets and made a body feel stiff.

  We'd been gone a couple miles and started making our way up the bank toward where it flattens out up on top of the hill to try and see exactly where we were. Usually we worked the other side of the river and knew little about this side, especially this far upstream, but we were together and it's always better to go about something unknown with someone else. We came up the hill to a fence and on the other side was a pasture. Down one direction of the fence was a house with a light, and in the pasture before the house was a heifer standing silhouetted. A big black one with dainty little horns.

She was rocking and nervous and I could tell there was something off about her but I couldn't see in the dark. We walked down the fence line and heard a grunting and moaning sound. Then we saw what was the matter. Ned Fischer was up behind this lonesome heifer standing on a stump, fornicating it quiet-like so his daddy couldn't hear from inside. He was going at it and his breath was coming out heavy and he had this face on where he looked real serious and was jutting his bottom lip down and showing his twisted bottom teeth. The heifer's narrow feminine hips didn't budge from the boy's rapid thrusts.

My chest was swollen and tight the way it gets when you know you're seeing something you shouldn't be seeing. That guilt fell heavy like a rock down my throat. Jaimie put the .22 to his shoulder and fired off a shot that zipped right over the heifer's head and sent the thing crazy. First, the cow let its bowels loose and defecated all over Ned, right up against his bare thighs and into his drawers that were around his ankles, then it bucked and kicked him off the stump he was standing on. Jaimie grabbed me by the shoulder and told me to run, but before we could turn, there was a calm smutty voice behind us in the thick weeds.

"You wanna ride, boys?' We spun and it was Ned's brother Yoho, standing there behind us with the eighteen-pound skinned coon carcass still warm and pink and leaky. Jaimie raised the gun again and shot right past Yoho's ear. I mean, he must have felt the sweat come off the bullet. Yoho fell to the ground holding his head and we crashed down the hill toward the river to lose him.

Yoho scratched his way to his feet and started after us. He picked his way like an ape down through the underbrush toward the river's edge and saw us, half swimming, half running through waist-deep water. Jaimie had the rifle over his head keeping it dry. He spun and shot another one at Yoho but that didn't stop him. He was crazed...trying to get shot, I guess. He was carrying the skinned coon by the jaw and holding it up and was yelling and hollering. That coon's pink tail was stiff and thin and pointy at the end.

We were about halfway across the river, a mile or so above the bridge. We didn't have to say it. In our boyhood panic we thought of one place and that was home. The shifting stones on the river floor rolled out from under our feet and our legs rolled out from under our bodies. I couldn't catch myself from falling. We were constantly fighting the strong winter current, but when we looked back, we saw Yoho standing at the edge of the water, seeming to forget about us, holding the coon out in front of himself and unclipping his overalls. We stopped in the middle of the river and looked at each other. Jaimie had wet hair and wide eyes; the moon so bright, it threw shadows that made the lines on his young face look desperate and deep.

Then, from the opposite bluff a shot rang out. I looked back at Yoho and he was ducking and running from the gunfire. Another shot hit the rock right behind his heel and he darted up the hill and out of sight. Another blast and the water exploded in front of me. I looked up and could make out what must have been a car one hundred yards away on top of the bluff. One of its headlights was missing. It was parked crooked next to a giant granite outcropping. Around the headlight there was a smaller light sort of bouncing like someone holding a lantern in his hand. I ducked down under the water and started to swim. My ears filled with that cold quiet water and I swam downstream and toward the bank. Another bullet ripped bubbles through the water in front of me. We were lucky that the car couldn't come farther down the bluff or the shooter could have come right up on us and picked us out of the water like ducks. I flopped up on the bank there tired and winded. For a second I didn't know which way was home. Coming up out of the water like that will get you turned around. When we were on the bankside, the gunman didn't have an angle on us. Jaimie took aholt of my hair and pulled me to my feet so as to get me going up out of the mud and sand and rock. Our jeans were covered in sand and we were wet but steaming because of all our body heat.

We ran the next mile home, Jaimie with the rifle down at his side, the Llano River dripping off of him. The whole way we didn't speak. When we got to the barn we undressed and built a fire to dry our clothes. I laid in the straw, staring at the fire. Jaimie fell asleep but I couldn't shake the fear of the bullets and the guilt of seeing what I saw. I thought who in the hell would have shot at us like that. First I thought it was Ned, but it couldn't have been Ned. If he'd crossed the river in a car he would have been coming from the Castell bridge and would have been on the east side of that outcropping. The next river crossing upstream was fifteen miles away and he couldn't have made it that fast. Whoever the shooter was, he came from the north side of the river and he wanted us and Yoho dead.

The next morning, I had to explain to my daddy that Jaimie and I'd been out so late because it had been a right lucky hunt, and we were killing a whole lot of coons until I took a spill in the river and my rucksack got washed downstream. He said that we'd go out that afternoon and look for it in case the skins got lodged against a log or a rock or got caught in an eddy. So we did, and the whole time I walked behind my father I acted like I was looking for the rucksack even though I knew the skins we were looking for were still walking around the river bottom wrapped tight around the bodies of some warm blooded coons.

I was dead tired from running all night and from walking the riverbank looking for the lost skins, but that afternoon there was work to be done on the farm. I felt distracted and companionless driving the tractor. I fell into a soft spot and had nearly gotten stuck, but made it out. I was lucky to be on dry ground but the wheels were congested and choked with mud, so I shut it down and knew I had to clear the muck out of the tires and the chassis.

After the engine was cut and the field is quiet again, and when you climb down and get close to the tires, the last thing to make a sound is the wet mud burping and popping while it settles into place. Mud is a bald challenge. It sticks heavy in the tracks of a machine like sandwich bread sticks to the roof of your mouth. The machine is built to move through mud and it did the job and wasn't sunk swallowed, but bogged from clogged hollows. You have to clean it so it can move again. So it can creak forward and gain steam.

Even in the hill country, you can get periods of prolonged rain, and that year we got wet. Land near the river or creek bottoms can become soft. I once overheard an old-timer German say that if you're going to work down around the Llano when it rains, you better grow webs between your toes. I pictured Ned and Yoho with grey webbed feet. They were built for this work and would never escape it.

The kind of mud we get is that black river loam that's great at holding moisture and great at mothering grass, and great at sticking to the guts of your tractor and rusting it out. I slid the shovel off the deck and it grated against the machine with an unclean industrial type sound. Tools always have an unwilling kind of look to them before they're forced into work. This one had a steel handle for added weight and solidity. With my hands wrapped unbroken around the handle I swung the shovel back, tipped my chest forward, turned my spine and slung my hands forward past my hip. I threw everything I had behind the tool and felt it slide to a stop somewhere deep inside the mud, slowed easy by the drag. That's what you want to feel. You want to hear the crunch of your shovel a foot or so deep. You want to put the blade up close to the steel without hitting anything square. You want to shave clean and narrow like you're aiming for chin hairs. You leverage the shaft against anything fixed, crank your wrist over and that black Texas mud thumps solid to the earth where little bluestem leaves vibrate in the wind around your feet like faith in motion.

You get good, too. You get high. A high from working, because you're good at working and you're liking it. With some punches of the shovel you pull out twenty, thirty pounds of mud at a time and it's building up around you in ugly piles that don't look natural but will wash down with rain, round out and flatten so wide. And the rain will do it in an instant too, it will do it in a month or so, and a month is an instant. You get older and start to realize a month is an instant.

You really aren't sweating until you miss your mark and throw that steel shovel against something fixed. All your heavy speed comes back at you and the shock shoots up the handle like a spike into your wrist, through your arm bone and out the back of your elbow, chasing rhythm out with it. Just, tick, full stop, and you feel you've been sweating. A dull tick. And that metal don't give. Just, tick. And all your fervor ricochets back and bounces around in your stomach like an embarrassment. The sun gets hot then, too.

You throw that shovel around, stabbing everywhere like a crow plucking meat from the ribs of a hot carcass, and your focus bleeds and you end up catching a piece of steel again. It's the surprise of it. That shock shoots longways through your wrist and you cuss and feel the sweat beads drive down the center of your chest between your pectorals. You judge mud by the way it sticks, and this stuff is relentless. There's a couple ways to get it from off your spade. I've heard hands say grease your blade, but that doesn't work. The best way is to let the mud sit overnight. Go do something else. Let it harden like rheum in the corner of your eye. Let it harden like the rest of the desert. It falls out easy then. But, I knew what my daddy would say if I told him I was letting his tractor sit dirty and the work sit undone.

    The next day was a Monday and that meant school. Jaimie and I greeted each other in the schoolyard without a gesture or a word. The memory of that boy was still heavy between us. We walked side by side into the classroom. The day went normal until and we had FFA after school. Clyde Yesper was also in FFA with Jaimie and me. We were standing around in the grass wearing our cowboy hats and boots, real forward-looking Texan boys. At least we looked it. On the inside I was still distracted. Clyde started up talking to the gang of us and at first I didn't pay much attention.

    "Yeah, my momma got shot Saturd'y night. They was master Mes'can marksmen tryin' to smooch her inheritance money she just got from my dead uncle in Wyoming. Not master 'nough though, cause they only clipped her in the arm so she be fine. They was just sitting in the car listening to the radio getting ready to go check the trot lines in the river. My daddy was in the passenger seat because, see, he can't drive on account of he's still got a lame foot, and my momma was in the driver's chair and the bullet came and busted the windshield and my momma looked all surprised and shot up, and my daddy took over and flopped her in the passenger seat with her screamin' and leakin', and drove downstream and caught them three snipers crossing the river to come gether their pay from my poor momma's cold white hands, but she wasn't cold nor white yet. No, she was alive.

    "You said Saturday night?" Jaimie asked.

    "Yes'ir. On the Llano. They must have staked us out for weeks, cause they knowed my momma been going down the river at night to check the trot lines by herself since my daddy got his foot trampled by a steer, and they knowed she kept the cash in the floorboard of the truck, but they didn't know my daddy was gonna be there that night to keep her comp'ny. They wasn't counting on two heads being there. Daddy says sometimes when snipers is shooting through a windshield the glass is enough to shake the bullet just a shade and that win'shield was German glass so it held up and knocked that bullet off kilter. Daddy just had a feelin' he wanted to go help his bride that night even though his foot wasn't no good and he wasn't any help 'tall. He still wanted to go just on a feeling he had. Just a wind. Well, I'm glad he had that wind, or else my momma mighta bled out and died. They musta been vet'rans from the war. Said they sneaked up river and shot from somewhere downstream and was working they way over to c'llect the body and the cash but they mustn't a figured for two people in the truck, cause he said they sure looked surprised when he was out there hobblin' on one foot, blasting at 'em in the river. My daddy knowed they was Mes'cans 'cause they was short little fellas, not quite the size of a white man, and they could swim like otters. One ran up the hill and the other two ducked under the river and got away."

I looked at Jaimie and he looked at me. I walked away from the group and around the back of the bleachers and vomited.

"You shot Clyde's momma," I said, when Jaimie came back around to look for me.

"Why'd you walk away like that?" he said looking back over his shoulder.

"How'd you just stay and listen to it?" I said.

"I had to wait around and hear some details in case we need to get our story right." I felt like I was going to fall over.

"You almost killed a woman."

"I know. I know. I shouldn't have done it, but I wasn't aiming for anyone. At least we know who was chasing us, now" he said.

"It sounds like they aren't suspicious on us. Just think it was a pair of crazy Mexicans," I said.

"Sounds like she'll survive," he looked around the bleachers to the boys still standing in a circle around the tall boy.

It was the first time in his life Clyde got the attention he was after. To this day, at house parties and rodeos you can hear the story of the trio of Mexican assassins on the Llano that tried shooting poor Mrs. Yesper down.

Jaimie looked at me and then down at the ground.

"She'll be fine." He swiped the bottom of his boot across the top of the grass, then looked up. "Might have to stuff that arm in the refrigerator, but she'll be fine," he said. He poked his bottom lip out and pulled his hat down to hide his eyes.

CHAPTER 12 ...
Dirty Work

He lied on his back under the rear axle of a green pickup truck, its dry-rotted tires so flat the metal rims were exposed. His ideas were jumbled but his words were lithe, and they came from someplace unseen underneath the muffler. I asked him about Steve, the Store's only employee besides Jennifer, hoping maybe the conversation would shine some light on Randy's past. Steve was a retired older man that only worked one night a week to offer Jennifer some relief. He had arthritic hands and an idle demeanor. If you stood near the bar long enough on the night Steve worked, you were liable to take a load of trash to the dumpster or restock the cooler for him.

"Steve's a flunky," Ickie said into the undercarriage of the broken down pick up.

"What's that?" I asked, handing him a socket wrench.

"A flunky? A flunky's this guy, when the boss skips out, gets all the authority. Just somebody the boss can trust that don't know a fuckin' thing and won't fuck nothin' up from tryin'. Whenever somebody come in and ask the flunky a question he just give 'em that look and they know, fuck it, come back another day. A no answer man. That's a flunky. Ain't got no answers. Boss'll pay him good, treat him good, send him on vacation, buy him lunch every once in a while. See, you're trained in school, be top notch y'know, get a good job and everythang. Well, there's a lot of good jobs for flunkies that don't know nothin'. Steve don't know nothin', don't act like he know nothin'. Nothin'. See, that type of person's valuable also."

"So, when Jennifer is out, Steve is just there to ensure that nothing gets done?" I said.

"And nothing gets done wrong," he said. "Randy actually hired him. Steve was all fucked up from a divorce late in life out in Mason and Randy could tell this guy's hurtin' so he gave him a job. Gave him some friends. Something to do."

"I get it."

"I still like the guy though. Most flunkies you don't like, but Steve's a cool dude," he said. "Tends bar but don't do nothing after that."

"He's one of my favorites," I said. "We just bullshit and talk baseball."

"He ain't dumb like I was sayin' with most flunkies. He's just old and tired and got the arthritis. Just don't want to talk to nobody about work."

I wasn't getting much out of Ickie, but seeing the ranch helped. I spotted a spade shovel and a tamp in the lean to while I was handing him tools and holding his lamp. Nothing up to that point in the memoir indicated any type of clue as to where Randy hid the money, but I needed as starting point. With over a thousand acres to search, I wasn't about to walk out to the middle of a field and start poking around so, that night, I picked a landmark, the barn. Under the moonlight, each hole I was a few feet deep and a few feet wide. I worked along the back wall of the barn first, then down both sides. When I was satisfied with a hole and determined it was bust, I filled it back in and tamped the ground, making sure to throw grass back over the disturbed soil. I must have dug a dozen or so and the sky started to glow with the morning sun. I gave it up and considered the barn tapped. I put the shovel and tamp back where I found them and walked back across the river, my hands throbbing. I knew I wasn't going to be able to sleep. The Store wouldn't be open for a while. I wiped my muddy boots in the grass before breaking in through the garage door and going up into the loft. Something good was bound to come up in Randy's high school years.

CHAPTER 13 ...
A Woman

Every bump and wiggle tugged on the old Dodge but the barrel racer was steady behind the wheel. She'd been driving since she was eleven and had already covered ten thousand miles with the horse trailer behind her. Inside the trailer stood her black and white appaloosa. Its fur was silky like a crow. Her daddy bought him on her first birthday. That May, she'd began her old horse's last circuit. One more good year.

Her black hair was unbraided and looked relaxed. It fell a long way down her back and almost sat in the seat with her. The hot concentrated breath coming through the cracked window made a few brave hairs dance on the edge of her mane. She had a maturity that she pressed onto friends and boys and male school teachers. We'd been driving for a few hours and I was staring through the window at the side view mirror. I could see the horse's snout as he pushed it through the bars of the trailer. The radio went silent. I looked over at her finger on the nob, then to her, but she never looked at me. She swallowed a dry gulp and took one hand off the wheel and fastened it into her lap, firm and still. She drove like that for a little while. The heat pulsed through me.

It was the summer after my senior year. She was a few years graduated. I'd broken my leg quarterbacking the varsity team that fall and it ended my athletic career so I fell full-fledged into farming and ag. I decided on Texas Tech and an agricultural economics degree. My friends and I hung out at every rodeo and county fair we could get to. We went to the auctions on Mondays just to stay up to date on prices and I won every FFA judging competition I entered.

At the rodeo in Llano that June is where I met the barrel rider. We went behind the food tent and kissed and fooled around. By then I knew what to do, but I didn't know what I was doing. That night, with the fiddle strings in the background she took my hand and asked me to come to Lockhart. I agreed. We made plans for her to pick me up in town. The whole week on the ranch, I couldn't stop thinking about her. On Friday, I met her in the empty parking lot of the high school and climbed in the passenger seat. It took about five miles before I had the courage to speak up but I managed polite conversation and even made her giggle once.

A few hundred miles later on some eastbound highway the instinct took over. Her hand was still in her lap. It was cupped and unmoving. I stared at it from the passenger seat without turning my head. She unbuttoned and lifted herself off the seat so her jeans could slacken a little. When she raised her hips off the seat her weight shifted to the gas pedal. The trailer thudded hard into the cracks on the highway. The girl's clean unpainted fingernails disappeared inside of her. That strange primal heat spread outward through my torso and felt like a bull stomping on my chest with a leg made of electricity. I sat there in the passenger seat just watching. We were entering Grape River, crossing into the little highway town at ninety-five miles per hour.

"Dang," she said out loud, braking quickly and putting both hands back on the wheel, her waistband still undone. The momentum pushed me to the edge of the seat. She finally slowed, and looked around. Contrition dulled my thoughts and sobered my shaking. The symbols of the small southern town were glaring and in some ways felt too obvious. We passed a hardware store, a dancehall, a diner, all innocent and non-contemplative.

She came to the town's one stop sign. A small community prayer garden sat empty along the side of the main drag in the smack middle of town. A footpath of half-buried stones led through a short wooden fence to a little white cross. The cross stood erect and humble in the grass, wedged tightly between two untrimmed rose bushes. The small roadside shrine shook her from her apathy and seduced her. She wasn't religious much but found it hard to be unaffected by the totems that people hold meaningful. The mystic impulse, to her, was impossible to refrain from. Not that she wanted to refrain from it. We kept driving.

The eyes of the small community hadn't been enough to kill it off. She wanted to finish. The horse's nostrils flared through the bars of the cage. The speed limit increased like it does when leaving all friendly places. The engine strained and pulled her thoughts back into openness. Our speed built and her fingers were in her lap again, and wet, just east of Grape River. Her foot fell on the gas. Faster. She was up to sixty-five. Her throat was open and dry. Seventy-five. She slid her hips forward and slouched lower in the seat spreading herself. The speed limit was eighty-five. We were pushing a hundred and I was eighteen years old and fully dressed. Her head rolled back and to the side and her eyes closed briefly. She whimpered because she was coming and breathing, and coming and breathing and coming over a hill at one-hundred fifteen miles per hour with her eyes closed. Exploding red and blue lights. A roadblock. Her eyelids opened lazily. A cop car was parked diagonally across both lanes. Two cars were stopped in a line behind it.

"Woah," she yelled. My heart tripped. Brakes locked and she slid, leaving hot black marks on the open highway. The horse and trailer coiled behind her. She fought to keep control of the truck. She locked her arms out stiffly holding the wheel. I reached forward and put my hands on the dash. We stopped a few inches short of the bumper of the second car.

A cop and a cowboy stood in front of the police car in the middle of the highway. They simultaneously turned their shoulders and looked back at the girl with the horse trailer, sliding to a stop. The cop towered over the man in the cowboy had by at least a foot, and he was much younger. After hearing no collision, they both turned back and looked toward Grape River Bridge, a small crossing a quarter mile down the highway.

In the truck, we didn't breathe for a minute. We didn't talk. Everyone stayed like that for a while. The cop and the old man stood side by side in the middle of the country highway with their arms crossed and nothing to say to one another. More cars came over the hill too fast but were able to stop, and a line grew behind the blockade. I could smell the wild onion grass that grew near the wet runnel outside the window. It was mixed in with burning oil and exhaust and hot asphalt.

Walking slowly to the first car in line, the old cowboy tugged the bottom of his shirt, straightening the wrinkles. The barrel racer and I watched as he had a talk with the driver. He did the same with the second car, tipped his hat then made his way to our truck. Her window was already down.

"There was a fatality on the bridge last night," he said after settling squarely next to her door. "The police are doing an investigation, measuring the tire marks and damage to the guardrail...things like that," he said turning his whole body to look east toward the scene of the crash. "The boys are trying to figure out exactly what happened."

"Jesus. How terrible," she said and looked out the windshield toward the squad of three or four government vehicles a quarter mile ahead.

"Yes, it is," the old man whispered, as if he was talking to himself. His expression was kind, though he didn't smile. The way his face formed words and phrases revealed a gentleness about him. He was distracted.

"You have a good day, Miss." He looked at us sadly. "And be safe."

He left us and continued down the line, explaining the hold-up through each driver-side window like it was some sort of obligation or like he didn't know what else to do. After another long wait, she saw in her rearview a truck driver climb out of his rig. He was a few cars behind us, and heavyset. He lumbered toward the officer. The barrel racer watched them chat for a minute until he began back to his truck.

"Do you know how long it's gonna be?" she asked the truck driver when he passed by her window.

"About fifteen to twenty," he said. His Spanish accent and soft face made him look almost childish. "That old man's granddaughter. She crashed last night. Sixteen," he said.

The racer looked back through her mirror and saw the old cowboy still talking to each car. He was a soul adept in courtesy and grace. The truck driver walked back to his spot in line. We sat in silence for a long time.

Then, the procession started slowly. She approached the bridge then crossed it, pulling her horse, on its last good year, atop clean black tire marks that screamed the night before. On the railing of the bridge hung a sad juniper wreath dressed with a spilling black bow, greasy under the hot Texas sun like a feather plucked from a living bird.

CHAPTER 14 ...

Hoochin' and Poochin'

I was done reading around 6 a.m. and went into the van and lied around in the heat for a few hours toying with the red poker chip, asking it for answers. That afternoon, Jennifer tapped on my door. She was wearing her Twisted Bitch hat. Her ex-husband, as he walked out the door, hurled the slur at her and it stuck. She was one twisted bitch. Divorced and broke at forty, she had to start again. All she kept in the divorce were the dogs, the breast implants and the nickname. The day I left Texas, the Twisted Bitch Cattle Company had forty-five head of Santa Gertrudis cattle across two ranches. There was Twisted Bitch wine, Twisted Kitchen Seasoning and a whole line of Twisted Bitch trucker hats that sold better than the beef.

"You wanna go hoochin' and poochin', Doodah?" she asked. I wiped my eyes. "Harlan's coming so put a shirt on. Don't want to make him nervous."

Jennifer didn't invent hoochin' and poochin' in the hill country, but everyone I asked said she coined the phrase. Originally, it started with her, a bottle of Deep Eddy vodka, her two dogs, Dixie and Dallas, and a sun-soaked Toyota Tacoma. The dogs went in the back, the vodka went in the passenger seat, strapped in with a lap belt, and the radio went to full blast.

The night I went hoochin' and poochin', though, there was no Toyota. Instead, her and Harlan pulled up to my van in two side-by-sides.

"Here, don't wreck it," she said as she stepped out of the ATV she was driving and plopped down next to her fiancé in the other. The vehicle sat in park, idling. Cane jumped into the bed and his nails pattered on the hard plastic. There was a bottle of Tito's Vodka in the bench seat with the belt wrapped snug around it. I pressed the brake and pulled the stick down into drive. We hit the red dirt roads. Harlan was driving the lead buggy with Jennifer in the passenger seat. Keeping my distance, I followed at the rear.

      The sun and I saw each other only in passing that day. But, what I did see of it simmered in nostalgia. Following Harlan on his driver's side rear, Cane and I ran parallel to a wall of dust. The sun sat on the other side of the chalky brown wall and smelled like exhaust fumes. The warm vodka smelled like high school and tasted like shit. I reached back and rubbed Cane behind the ear. I wasn't afraid of the law. I wasn't afraid of doing any more damage because when you live on the bottom a fall is just a scrape on the hands.

      Eventually, we got drunk and it got dark. About seven miles away from home, we were grinding along at about 11 m.p.h, a pace so slow that Jennifer's hair-sprayed hair hardly fluttered at all. Both ATVs had their radios tuned to the same station so we could ride next to one another like a late-night hill country block party on wheels. I pulled around to the passenger side to smile drunkenly at Jennifer. She smiled back and tugged on Harlan's shirtsleeve rested her chin on his jawbone and yelled something into his ear. His eyes stayed in a squint and they slowed to a stop. I did the same. All the dogs were lying down in the back of each rattling vehicle, bored and sober. Jennifer got out and stumbled in the sand and worked her way carefully around my side-by-side, holding onto the hood, and slid into the passenger seat. Harlan was messing with the radio and didn't realize his foot wasn't on the brake. He was creeping slowly toward the side of the road, and into a ditch. The bumper crunched at the bottom the soft sandy ditch and a prickly pear cactus bush butted its way into the cab with him.

"I've Come to Expect it From You" by George Strait came on and she pressed my knee and ordered me to put it in park.

"Can you two-step?"

"I can't even step," I said. She took me by the hand and walked me around to the front of the buggy. She told Harlan to go down the road and turn around and face us. The red road gleamed in the headlights. We tried to dance and fell over one another and laughed our way through the rest of the song until she had to pee. I walked over to Harlan in the other vehicle. He turned the music down.

"How long you gonna be in town?" he asked. I could tell the fiancé was uneasy with me around. Especially since he lived a hundred miles away and I was sleeping in the Store's backyard.

"I guess until Jennifer tells me to go," I said.

"Lotta work left?" he asked and swigged the bottle and tightened the cap without offering any to me.

"That loft is dense with shit but I haven't really worked on it much lately. She's got me doing other stuff," I said. "And I'm helping Ickie every once in a while, too."

"I'll be honest, I'm glad she got you working up there and not me. She's been fooling around up in that loft for months," he said.

"She goes up there?" I asked and burped.

"Yeah she does but don't nothing change when she comes down. I think she naps up there," he said.

"She's going through Randy's old things?" I asked.

"If she is, she's just moving them from one place to another. It ain't like her to do something dumb like that. I think she sleeps up there," he said repeating himself the way a drunk person will do. But I knew something her fiancé didn't. I knew what she was really doing up in that loft. She was reading the memoir. But why send me up there? Why not keep the money a secret? Jennifer came out of the bushes buttoning her jeans.

"You boys getting along?" she asked. We nodded and I walked back to my buggy. Maybe she couldn't find the money and was seeing if I could crack it. That made sense. She parked me behind the Store so she could keep an eye on me. We loaded up and headed home, careful not to tip.

The next morning, I walked into the Store. Harlan was there and Jennifer had made breakfast in the bar's kitchen. Enough for all three of us. I no longer wanted her near. I didn't want her watching me, keeping an eye on all my movements. What happened when I found the money? Was she going to shoot me?

"I think I'm going to park the van on the north side of the river today," I said. "Get out of y'all's way."

"No that's dumb. Where you gonna park it?" she asked.

"I think down in that lot in front of Randy's old place. You know I fell asleep on the river bank when I first got here. I feel more connected to the river down there," I said.

"Don't start that hippy shit this early in the morning while I got a headache," she said.

"It's true," Harlan said. "I saw him sleeping in the rocks when I was fishing that day. If the boy wants to get out of the nest let him go. Gotta get off momma's teet." He said, pointing at her implants with his dirty fork.

"She smacked him in the back of the head and his Twisted Bitch hat fell in his hash browns and ketchup.

"That's horseshit. You'll stay here, Doodah. The river floods this time of year. You'll get washed away," she said.

"No, I think I'm going to go. I haven't fished once since I've been here. I need to get out of the city."

"Castell is not the city, dumb dick," she said. "It's an old blacksmith's shop and a parking lot."

"I like Doodah better," I said. Harlan laughed. I didn't have her approval but she couldn't stop me, really, without making a big scene. That afternoon I moved the van to the mud parking lot on the other side of the river near the bridge. If I was going to find what I was looking for, I was going to have to start on the north bank of the Llano. That night I made a fire near the water's edge and stared into it wishing I could sing a song. I thought in lyrics. Like a marshmallow, my song melted above the flame tips.

If I could play guitar I'd write a song about Texas, and all the places I've never been. It would be about Texas and these river rapids that hush me to sleep. It would be about caramel-colored snakes, and this wood that I've cut and this fire that burns my chili. It would be about the geese, a thousand miles high that make me feel small, and sandpipers that make me feel ugly.
Teach me to blow a harmonica and I would sound like this wind ripping through the mesquite trees. I would whistle about the owls, solitary in their service.

I would write about the Comanche and their slaughter and I'd groan nervous like every southern scholar and heart-broken child. I'd sing about the millionaires I've met. I'd pluck along to their envy because they know they can't buy twenty-three and they can't croon wild like me. My voice would be a sweet bumpy crackle, from a natural Northern cracker, and it would sound exactly like yours does in your head. It would make the coyotes hush and the wolves would pay $5-a-head to sit around my fire.

My songs would sizzle inside of you like a burning cigarette in a windless room. My songs would tell you things you already know. They would make promises. My guitar would kick you in your teeth and confuse you like this rain I'm pouring, and these beans I'm frying, and this airplane I'm crashing and this book I'm writing and this stranger I'm dancing beside on the streets of San Angelo at sundown under carnival lights. Put this song in your razor blade pocket and forget about it. My songs are all sad ones, deep and correct. Upon hearing them, the lion lays down his hat and traces shadows in the sand.

The bottom of my boots are flattened and I've seen each coast, because there are only two, the one in front of you and the one in back. If I had a guitar I'd name it "The Mutt." I'd wear a t-shirt with a picture of a roller skate on it. My songs would be for poets but they wouldn't give a damn. You'd sing my songs on your lunch break and to your newborn son. My songs would make you give up all this working and learn the guitar, too.

My dog and I would live on the cheap under the misshapen trees along the river. They'll bud again and grow sideways, but they'll strain and reach upward with an aching back. Cane and I would share breakfast and dinner. I'd put him in my songs. I'd let him drive when I got tired and he'd fetch me my ducks when I shot them. My songs would trudge along even after you've lost interest in them, the same way a baseball game takes patience to watch.

I would scratch my lyrics onto napkins and carve them into trees and in time they would fade and disintegrate along with the rest of the world's stories. So, maybe I won't learn the guitar and just forget this fire, call it a wrap, and get back to digging.

CHAPTER 15 ...

Forgiveness

One day, tired of oatmeal, I drove into Llano for breakfast. When I pulled into The Hungry Hunter my phone began to buzz with voicemails and text messages. I'd gotten a text from my sister telling me that my lawyer had called again in St. Louis, and that she was trying to get ahold of me. The fear of the repercussions finally capsized whatever comfort I found in avoidance and I decided to call. It rang twice and the attorney picked up. Her voice carried sympathy and command at the same time, and the sound of it shot memories of the courtroom through the speaker and into the animal half of my mind.

"Luke, I hope you are well. I have some news for you, and it's been a long time coming since it's been so difficult to get into contact. Anette Parker, the state's key witness in your case, reached out to my office inquiring about you."

Whenever I hear her name I imagine her writing body in the driver's seat, the nerves in her spine sparking and failing to connect.

"Is she suing me?" I asked.

"I don't believe so. If she were filing a civil case, she would have started the process by now, and it would have been a lawyer calling, not the plaintiff. She just said she'd like to speak with you. She wants to meet with you in person if you are available and willing."

"Tell her I'm out of the state. Out of the country." There was a pause.

"I can't advise you on how to conduct your personal affairs, Luke. All I can do is pass on the message. I can't be sure, but usually when this happens, it is the victim showing mercy to the defendant. She is doing you a favor. She wants to forgive you. I'm not going to call her back. I think you should. If she calls again I will tell her that you're out of the state, but I have a feeling this call is one you want to answer."

"Is that all?" I asked.

"Yes," she said. I hung up the phone, flicked my cigarette into a flower pot and walked inside to order breakfast with a shaky voice. More than ever, I wanted to dig. I wanted to find that money and leave the country. I thought about a drive to South America. Pieces of Randy's early life had failed to trigger a sign. I was no closer to finding the money than when I started. That day was a Monday, and the Store was closed, so I thought I'd get some reading in. Back in Castell, I busted into the Store and came across a story that caught my attention. It was Randy's first summer back home after his freshman year of college.

CHAPTER 16 ...
Hidden Ball Trick

On campus at Tech, I drove a 1963 Volkswagen Beatle because my father wanted something German made, and when I was back home in the summer I liked the look of it and I liked the attention it brought. Though when I made hardware deliveries for Mr. Buttery I drove the company Ford. The old F-100 pickup rattled and spat and was built for hard work.

I just got off my shift and had the truck for the night. I pulled it into the gravel parking lot next to the ball field and parked it, picked up my straw Stetson that sat in the passenger seat and slid it back over my hair. I had hair, then. I was the only one in the whole park. I reached up on the dash and grabbed the flask that was sitting under the window and took a swig.

I got out of the driver's seat and reached into the bed of the pickup. There was a tarp in the back covering some scaffolding that I had to deliver to a jobsite the next morning. I pulled back the tarp and heaved out the grey canvas bag full of bats and baseballs. It gave off that powdery baseball smell which straightened my head a bit. I walked across the rocky parking lot. The rocks crunched under my boots. The bats clanked together in the bag. The simple field next to that simple parking lot was a shallow sandy reprieve from the immodesty of my college years. It was an open stage waiting to host something spectacular. It was truly American. When I sat in the dugout alone, the chipped green paint on the bench had a pattern to it that was chaotic but natural and familiar to me. The chain-link fence fit easily into the folds of my fingers when I reached for it. Sitting on the bench I took off the hat and held it down between my knees. My pale white midsummer forehead hurt from the inside. The dry evening breeze worked to cool the damp band of leather inside the hat.

Players started to file in. The ones who lived in town walked, the others caught a ride or biked. There's a strange magic about the way boys come together dressed in uniform. They're like metal fillings under a magnet. They're a haphazard mess, but then they arrive at the ballfield and seem to all straighten out and look to belong in accordance. When they change back into street clothes at the end of the afternoon they fall apart again, just a gaggle of dirt-faced yokels, all sloppy and disordered walking home toward a hazy setting sun with leather mitts balanced on their heads. Even if a team is short a player and someone's younger brother steps in, or you poach a kid from the other team just so you'll have eight, the uniform works its authority. The minute he's dressed, he looks as if he was always meant for it. His crooked hat floats among the others in the dugout, his spikes crunch like all the rest on the concrete floor. His holler from the outfield does its part to contribute to the lazy racket of a baseball diamond in summer.

They all played catch and pickle and flips to waste time until the umpire showed. Every week, Chuck Borshette, the live-in jailer, umped the games and every week we had to wait to start while his wife fed the inmates an early dinner.

One year, Mr. Borshette shot a buck on the Laderly farm. And it was a big deer, too. One of the heaviest on record in Llano County. Mrs. Borshette made chili out of the deer and every night for a month she fed the six occupants of the Llano County jailhouse the same hot red slop. A little cruel, but Mr. Borshette maintained that the meal was cheap on taxpayers, and there ain't nothing in the books that says you have to offer a criminal a thriving diet. After a month of deer chili, them boys was keeled over and hurting and right depressed and malnutritioned from all the hot meat and no greens, until finally, one night, a bright salad showed up on the mess hall table. It was a sign that they'd eaten their way through the biggest deer in county history, which was a feat they accomplished with hung heads. That salad left them upbeat and contented, though. The next morning, the six cons woke up to a seventh. Sometime in the middle of the night, a new prisoner had arrived. A slick haired out-of-towner. Naturally, they watched him, studied him and were mighty occupied with him until dinner. And that night the red deer chili was back. The inmates groaned and spat on the floor and refused to eat. Looking down into his bowl, the new inmate asked what was wrong with the chili.

An old con turned to him. "Ain't nothing wrong with it on the first night."

"Lucky me. I'm only here for a night," the stranger said. "Borshette told me they only hold drunk drivers for a day, and since no one was hurt, I'll be on my way to San Antone tomorrow, as long as I pay for damaged property."

"What'd you hit?" the old inmate asked.

"I went through a fence. Hit a deer standing in the middle of a pasture. He was a big bastard. Borshette said it might take the record."

The kids were bored of flips and started to get fidgety. Most of them had found their way back into the dugout with me and were starting trouble the way boys will do if they're asked to wait.

"You got a girlfriend with big tits, Randy?" one of the dirty faces asked me. It was Perry our second baseman and younger brother to the shortstop, Mac. I let him play up a year because he was a decent little infielder and worked naturally with his brother up the middle. But he was rowdy and raunchy and had a shit-starting disposition. Some boys on the team were meek, and I understood that to be their nature, but others, like Perry, were good company and liked to stir things up. It seemed that the latter type was more interested in girls so I helped them where I could. It was my duty to instill Southern values in them boys. I was developing them into men, future leaders. So, I wouldn't just teach them baseball. I'd tell them how to drink, fill them in on women and the delicate art of chasing them.

"I got a couple of them, Perry," I said. They all went ooooh, and laughed. "I ain't chicken shit with girls the way ya'll are," I told him. "You ever heard of the cattle guard game? It's a little game I made up here in the hill country. And I might say this is the best place in the world to play it," I said. That lit them up. They was so inquisitive about that one.

"What's the cattle guard game, Randy?" they asked. "It goes like this," I said, standing in front of them like a lecturer at Tech. "You load up your truck with a cooler full of ice and beer, and ride around on backcountry roads with some chick and drink that ice cold beer. That sounds like a good time in itself, but it gets better because every time you run over a cattle guard you both have to finish your beer and take off a piece of clothes." That had them teeming. "I know every back road and every cattle guard in Llano and Mason Counties. I know a route that could have a chick totally naked before the radio hits a commercial break," I said. They laughed that ugly teenage laugh, loud and snorty. "Yeah, I'm picking two girls up tonight, after the game. They want to learn how to play." I wasn't lying either. There was a girl from Fort Worth I met at Tech. She had a friend whose uncle lived in Loyal Valley and they were coming out to the country to visit, and I told them that when they did, I'd show them how country boys rode the cattle guards. It was the age of free love. The 60s. The boys were all ears.

"At Tech," I said, "we'll find these girls at a bar and get to talking to them. We'll take them over to a guy's house. Twenty or thirty guys will have sex with her. They want it. One night we picked up this gal, and took her to this guy's house and drew numbers to see who'd go first. I drew number twenty-two." I told them about some of my other exploits at Tech. I told them about how I almost got suspended my first year for riding around with some rowdy boys at night killing deer and selling the jerky on campus.

Them stories got the boys bustling like a bunch of snakes and they spilled out of the dugout onto field laughing with new energy. Two boys were walking side-by-side across the third base foul line and I heard one of them say to the other, "Look, Scoots, we hit a cattle guard," and he swooped the kid's hat off his head and ran into centerfield, the other boy chasing him.

I saw that Mr. Borshette was finally making his way toward the field. I pulled a stained bar napkin out of my pocket and looked over the batting order I'd come up with that morning. The middle infield brothers were still on the bench lacing their spikes.

"Mac, you're leading off, playing short. Perry, you're in the nine hole playing second."

"What the hell, Randy! Why'm I always battin' last?" the fiery little kid asked.

"I like you and your brother back to back," I said.

"That's bullshit. Hit me second then."

"I ain't doing that."

"Why?"

"'Cause you ain't worth a shit yet, bub," I said looking down at him. The word yet was a compliment enough. You don't give direct compliments to your boys. It twists their heads. Baseball is all about shaving the edge off of the nerves. "Land one in some grass today and I'll move you up. How's that?" He spat brown tobacco through the fence next to him. I walked around the field telling the boys where they were playing and where they were batting in the lineup.

The game started and my buzz faded a little. If you ain't used to watching young kids play ball, you might get frustrated about how they move s'damn thorny and slow. After a while, though, your eyes get habituated to the speed of it, and the gawky dragged-out play starts to look fine, almost polished, as long as the out is made. They'll hit a groundball that takes all afternoon to reach the shortstop, he'll crouch down and fumble it, stand up, step towards first, and trip over his feet; the same two feet he's had his entire life, but all of a sudden now they're giving him trouble. He'll muscle up a long lob across the infield but the runner's skinny legs ain't developed yet either so they take a while to get moving. The runner looks like a locomotive with square wheels. His elbows are pumping, his running legs swing and flail out to the sides. Meanwhile, the throw from short is floating like a cloud towards first. The first baseman's standing there, spread-legged and frozen watching the heavy ball sail toward him. It thuds into his palm and beats the runner by a step. Alright, one down. I clap all enthused.

"Two more, here. Come on, now," I yelled from the dugout. We were getting beat through five. A hot grounder got by Perry up the middle, right under his glove, which scored two in the third. Then a fly ball fell in right-center and they scored another two. Not looking good. The game proceeded the way it does when you're losing under a broiling sun. It was the ninth inning and we were still down four. Little Perry lead it off and he beat one into the ground. It was one of those balls that took its time getting to someone's glove and Perry was a quick little guy so he beat it out. Then, with his older brother up to bat he stole second on the first pitch easy. When he popped up from his slide he jammed his shoulder into the shortstop's ribs.

"Oh, sorry, bub." He patted the fielder's back. "Stay off the bag next time," he said. As soon as the pitcher had the ball, he started stretching a huge lead taunting the kid. On the next pitch, Mac hit one square. A line drive that one-hopped just short of the center fielder. The ball was hit so hard it got there before Perry even touched third. The little guy came squirting around the corner looking home. The throw was already coming into the cut-off man. I was holding up my arms yelling at him to stay at third but he zipped right past me.

He was a little bug, a runt, but fast. You know the type. Wiry and mean and quick moving but can't do much damage. The first baseman took the cut, spun and flipped the ball to the catcher and Perry was still halfway up the line. The catcher stood as tall as a grown man, the biggest one on their team, a hog, holding the ball inside his mitt against his stomach. His feet were squared with the line and he was blinking dumbly inside his catcher's mask. Perry finally made it home and right before he reached the plate he ducked down and rammed the top of his head into the catcher's groin. Perry's head skipped off the kid's jock and he fell forward down in between the catcher's spread legs. The twit's face landed on home plate and above him the big catcher folded in half and fell backwards, his ass landing square on the back of Perry's head.

"Yer outta here!" the umpire yelled down at the scene. Perry came up gasping and dazed and fell back over. We didn't know much about concussions back then. "Go home, Perry," the jailer said to him. "That's a dirty trick. Not again. I ejected you last week, I'll do it again." Perry zig zagged slowly back to the dugout and sat at the end of the bench. There was a puddle of tobacco juice staining the middle of home plate. The umpire kicked the pool of spit and smeared it with the bottom of his shoe. "No, I said go home, kid," the umpire yelled toward our dugout.

"Chuck, he just got sat on, let him catch his breath," I yelled back. The game picked back up and the last two outs were quick. We lost the game leaving Mac stranded on second. I walked over to our dugout from third base glad the whole thing was over. I looked around for Perry but he was gone. The kids were all packing up changing back into jeans and t-shirts when I called their attention. "Does anybody know what Perry did wrong? He did something really stupid that you don't do in the game of baseball. Did anybody catch it?" They all looked around at each other. "This ain't gonna be one of those things, like school where everybody is too shy to speak up. That's boyish, and we're all men here. Don't be afraid to say it if you think you know the answer. Come on," I said. "Nobody can tell me what he did wrong on the bases there?" One of the boys lifted his eyes out from under the bill of his cap. Tucker Barne, our flat-footed third baseman spoke up, "He rammed his head into the fellas pecker, and then he got tossed."

"No." I said. "Anybody else?" No one spoke up. "When you're down four in the ninth inning, you don't run into an out at home plate. At that point, you chip away. You get men on base, you move them around, you hope something lucky happens. Some momentum. We were set up fine. Our nine-hole got on base then we had the top of the lineup coming up. Mac, Tucker, Simpson, with no outs. We were going to need more than Perry's one run to win, we were going to need five or six more hits that inning. There's no difference between losing 4-0 and losing 4-1." My speech stopped abruptly. I realized I was yelling at every kid besides the one that actually needed it. And as they were all staring up at me, waiting to go home and forget about the entire day, I realized that I had no reason to be upset either. I still had my postgame rendezvous with the girls from Fort Worth and life was good. "Alright, I'll see ya'll next week," I said.

I loaded all the gear up in the bag and met Chuck out at home plate while the kids were packing up and bumming rides home. The kids on bikes rode with little energy, their front tire unenthusiastically swinging from left to right as they struggled to gather speed up the parking lot hill.

"That kid's gon' leave somebody nutless," the jailer said.

"Trust me, I know. I'm gonna leave him nutless if he keeps fucking around and running through my signs."

"You might consider sittin' him next week, maybe even cuttin' him all together. Show him he can't do that," he said.

"Yeah I gotta do something."

"Careful goin' home. Keep that whiskey low," he said.

"Vodka," I said. I threw the bag of bats and balls in the bed of the pickup on top of the faded canvas tarp. I needed more hooch for the girls and I knew where I could find some. There was a pasture next to my folks' house full of white prickly poppy and at the corner of that field was a square fence post and under that post was buried three bottles of vodka. I put them there to hide from my mother. Pink and orange was the colors of the sunset that night while I pulled my truck through the gate on the northeast corner of the wildflower pasture. From where I was no one in the house could see me. There was a shovel in the bed of the work truck and when I threw the tarp back to look for it, I saw a body. Little Perry was curled up under the matt. I jumped back like he was a snake.

"What in the hell are you doing, kid?" I yelled. He jumped right down out of the back and into the field of white flowers.

"I wanna see some college tits, Randy!" he said, and punched me in the hip bone. He was pining to see something raunchy that night and I can't blame him. I swatted him and a cloud of dust discharged from the side of his head.

"Get in the truck," I said. He moped and walked around to the passenger seat thinking his fun was over. He had a round head too big for his body and big brown eyes and a little nose with freckles on it. "No, not the front seat. Get in the back, get the shovel." The tarp made him cough a high-pitched cough while he rummaged through the truck bed. "See where there ain't no flowers by that post there? Dig around until you hit something solid." I leaned up against the truck with my arms crossed and watched him jump up and down on the shovel. The crickets groaned and there were cool patches in the west wind. I could see where the boy's forehead sweat had turned the dust into paste. Soft loose soil held the crate in the ground. It wouldn't have taken me much effort to pull it out of the ground but the boy was tired and underfed so he labored to do it. In his small hands the crate looked like a coffin. He opened the lid and took out a bottle of vodka for me. "Good, now bury it and make sure the ground looks flat." He did and by that time it had gotten dark. "Get in the back," I said.

    We went and picked up those girls. I knew the one from Tech was going to be cute but goddamn her friend was hotter than a fucked fox in a forest fire. Every cattle guard had us stripping and taking shots. And Little Perry was discreet. A real gentleman in the truck bed. I hit a grate on Keyserville Road and the hot friend slipped off her blouse and was in her bra. When I got a glimpse of them tits in the moonlight I slammed on the brakes. I heard a thud in the bed of the truck. The sound of little Perry's head slamming into the sheet metal. I threw it in reverse and backed up over the cattle guard again. They weren't expecting that trick but weren't opposed to it either. The girls giggled and off came their bras. I never once saw the kid's head pop out from under the tarp. Not for air, not for light. But I knew he must've seen what he came to see because ever since that night he acted different on the ball field. A little more mature, a little more composed. Almost alert in a way, and cautious. Those titties stamped some character on him.

CHAPTER 17 …

Love, Anna

I set the page on the desk in the loft and leaned back in the busted chair. I knew the field of wildflowers he was talking about. I knew the exact fence post. If he buried liquor there as a college kid, the money could be there also. It was his spot.

Disturbed soil is easy to distinguish, and when I walked across the pasture that night with my shovel and tamp and dog, and stopped in the corner of the field, the ground looked hard and natural. Nothing was upturned or discolored. No one had been there recently.

I pressed the tip of the shovel into the soil and envisioned the money. The moonlight made my hands look grey. After an hour of digging, my spade thudded against something solid. My heart felt hollow. I bent my back and ran the bottom of the shovel's blade across the top of the wood, scraping off the light crumbs of soil. I carved around what I could feel was the edge of the crate. Each meticulous peck of the shovel, exposed more and more smutty wood. I reached down and the soil and rocks slid and clipped against one another as I pulled on the wooden box. The rotten top crumbled in my hands as I pulled away pieces of soft wood. Inside were a few rusty screw drivers and wrenches lying across one another. On top of those was a pad of prescription slips. Little square sheets of paper tightly stacked and yellowed at the edges presented a professional font. The shape of the letters reminded me of old military stationery from the Korean War that I'd seen at army surplus stores. From the office of Dr. J.M. Welds it said across the top. The first slip was written on in two different colors of ink. The first, in blue, was a note in the RX box that said: *Happy Birthday, Randy! To laughter... Love, Anna.*

In the doctor's signature line across the bottom in black ink was the practiced signature of Dr. J.M. Welds. There must have been forty or fifty blank slips in the stack.

CHAPTER 18 ...
Di

In college, I'd messed around with a few dozen girls, and after college I had my fun in Houston but I always knew none of them would stick. There was a time when I thought I could go on forever without a steady gal. But, Di came along and she was good, like really good. I had just been promoted at The Superior Oil Company helping Mr. Clack raise and sell cattle to sweeten land easement deals. It felt like I was somebody. Born on a ranch, feeding jackrabbits to hogs, and now I'm a big wig. I loved the way I looked in a tie and I loved the money. Di was the daughter of a client of mine. An oilman who ranked as the top golfer at his country club and handed his talents down to his only child. Di didn't want any of her daddy's money and she didn't take it neither. We were made for one another. Our blemishes fit together perfectly.

"Have you showered today?" I remember asking her from the bed in her small house in Houston. She was standing naked in front of the record player fingering with the needle.

"No."

"Have I?" I asked.

"I don't think so," she said.

"You want to shower?"

We were already undressed so we filed into the bathroom. The sewage line was busted somewhere under that house and the landlord didn't have the money to pay a plumber so we put up with it for the first year we were together. It smelled like stale water and ass. We stood in front of the mirror until the water got hot. She was behind me standing on her toes resting her chin on my shoulder. My arms dangled at my sides. I arched my back and sank into her. She reached under my arms and held my shoulders. The muscles in my torso were strained and showed in the sweating mirror.

"I get fatter in the evenings," I said. "In the morning, you could see the ripples in my stomach."

"No…It just sticks out at night since it's full of cud," she said taking one hand off my shoulder and running it down my chest and over my abdomen. She pressed her cheek against mine. "It's all working its way through there. All that pie's in there. It's in there," she pointed and opened her eyes acting like she was concerned.

"You put it in there," I said.

She kissed my ear and we looked at each other in the mirror. The sewage rose out of the pipes.

"You know, this smell will always remind me of you," I said, and turned to face her. And it has reminded me of her over the years. Even when I was remodeling a home with my second wife, and we punctured a line and got covered in shit. I was covered in memories of that little busted house on the south side of Houston rolling around, laughing with Di. Those are the kinds of promises you make to a woman that you keep, the private little vows that linger long after you've left them. The shower got hot and we got in.

We were standing so close together.

"Do you see me?" I grabbed her face and pulled it back away from mine.

"I see you."

"I just want you to see me right here in front of you." I kissed her. The water on her lips made the kiss slippery and hard to find. Her mouth was the wrong temperature.

We both looked down at the water rolling over my stomach. I never ate dessert before I met Di. I grew up in a house without sweets. You should eat a meal and be right satisfied with it but that ain't how she worked. It didn't matter how much she ate, she always had room for something sweet, and she stayed narrow all her life. Dessert was her only vice. Dessert and competition. Boy, was she competitive. When she was a kid there was always a cake or a pie or a plate of cookies on the counter waiting agreeable after every meal. And after she grew into a woman and moved out she took the habit with her. When we first started going together my moderation was a burden on her. I wouldn't go in for dessert and she had to find it on her own. She must have felt shameful eating desserts all alone like that. But, eventually, I grew keen on sugar too. After a few months, when we'd be out to eat I'd kind of pick at her chocolate or her ice cream after dinner and started wanting a bowl of my own. She turned me. It was more convenient for her to have gotten me hooked on the sweets. Addictions are easier with a partner. An accomplice doubles your efforts. It's like a junkie couple stealing and coning and chasing the high together. I'd get up from reading and fix two plates of pie, one for us both, without thinking.

"Today we had dessert after breakfast, dessert after lunch and I guarantee you'll have some of that lemon blueberry pound cake tonight," I said with squinty eyes as the little beads of water bounced off the top of her head and into my face.

"If there's some left, yes, I will have some. Yes," she said, soaping her arms.

"You're a full-blown adult dessert addict," I said.

"I am not an adult dessert addict. I'm only twenty-five." And it was true. At that point we'd only ever been young. When we were out of the shower the floor felt cold and wet under my feet.

"Can you comb my hair since the mirror's all foggy?" I asked her. She took the comb from me and ran it back through my hair. She'd seen me do it so many times she knew which direction to push each part. We were almost eye to eye as I leaned on the sink and she stretched her thin body as tall as it would go. Her eyes scanned the top of my head as she worked the comb and I watched her focus on me. I knew I would marry her.

"When you wash it, it lies flatter," she said, her breath right in my nose. The smell of her breath was even better than the sewage.

"Yeah, I don't like that. That's why I keep it dirty for a few days," I said. "I have to cash in on those days. I plan entire meetings around them." I ducked to the bottom corner of the mirror to get a glimpse, then kissed her head and went to lie back down.

"What are you doing, brushing your teeth?" I asked from the bed.

"Yes," she said from in the bathroom. I heard the water in the tub turn back on.

"What now?"

"Shaving my leg," she said. "I couldn't do it with you in here. You were in my way."

"Which one?" I asked.

"Right."

"How many more you got left?"

"Three more," she said. I laughed and watched the ceiling fan turn.

"What are you doing now?"

"Brushing my hair. Why you keep asking?" Her voice was jingly.

"Just need to know in case you're incapacitated one day and I have to fill in."

She came into the bedroom and curled up into me. We were lying all crissed and crossed.

"Don't your brain have electricity running in it?" I asked and pressing my forehead against her temple.

"Yeah. Everyone's does."

145

I hiccupped. "You think I'm gonna get zapped?" I asked.

"I wouldn't do that to you," she said looking down, smiling, picking at a thread on the blanket. "Plus, there's a lot of water and bone and meat and insulation to keep it from getting out."

I hiccupped again. "Goddamn, I can't shake these hiccups," I said. "Scare me."

"I wouldn't do that, either."

"Come on, I'm asking you to."

"No."

"Come on, Di."

"Knock it off."

"Make me flinch."

"No."

"Come on."

"I'm pregnant." I recoiled back into the couch and stared at her in silence. Then hiccupped. We were engaged a few weeks later.

It's been said that every man in Texas is an oilman, and that means me. I worked for The Superior Oil Company but I didn't have anything to do with the oil production or drilling. I just spent their money entertaining. My boss, Mr. Clack used cattle to get oil concessions in places like Indonesia, South Africa, South America and anywhere else his men could find it. If Superior Oil wanted to drill on some poor rancher's farm in Brazil we would offer them a fair price for the oil underground, but on top of that, we'd give them my cattle. These were Santa Gertrudis cows and bulls with the best bloodlines in Texas and that meant the best in the world. Now, the farmer not only gets money for the drilling rights but a herd of cattle so stout and profitable that his sons and grandsons could stay rich all their lives.

It takes a good eye to find and produce the best cattle in the world. With about thirty employees on three ranches all across Texas, I was running the whole show. We had 1,500 head. We're talking the best of the best; better than the King Ranch who had a 100,000. We weren't just there to give away animals. We had to sustain, so we sold cattle to other ranches too. This was my job, and I was good at it. If someone came to the ranch to buy a bull, by gad they bought a bull. I was a talker. A salesman. You have got to get the people to trust you. It's all about trust.

One night, Di and I got dressed up and drove down to the Shamrock Hilton in Houston. Inside the ballroom were men in Stetsons and suits. This was the seventies so the suits were every different color of an Amarillo sunset. Orange ones, maroon ones, pink ones. The wives were in evening gowns and the smell of their perfume mixed in with the heavy punch of smeared cow shit. Zip, the black cowboy that worked on my Houston ranch was waiting backstage with bull 4-6003 who had a halter around his snout. I shook hands with CEOs, politicians, journalists and professional athletes. In the background of the party, horses, sheep, pigs and cows walked across a stage on the south wall of the room. Some paid close attention to the sale but most folks were there to socialize.

We had a spot near the stage where we could see the bidding. I was walking back from the bar with Di's martini and two plates of cheesecake when I saw Zip escorting bull 4-6003 across the stage. I stopped and turned to watch. The muscles rolled in his shoulders and neck and it almost made me shudder. The bull's weight appeared in electronic numbers above the stage. I set one slice of cheesecake on the table in front of my wife.

"That come with the bull?" she asked.
"It comes with me," I said.
"Did you drop some off at your nurse's table too?"
"What?"
"I saw Anna Hensch here, the nurse you spend so much time with. I don't know why she'd fuck you when she's

got that handsome husband of hers. He's a ball player. You just roll around in cow shit." She took a cigarette out of her purse, lit it and pushed the cheesecake away.

"The bull looks good under these lights," I said.

"Yes, he's a big boy," she said.

There were over five-hundred people in the ballroom. After all the bulls had been staged, I went into an office near the exit where they told me 4-6003 had been sold for $40,000 to someone named Charles Keating. Di saw him coming before I did. I turned to see what she was looking at and a tall middle-aged man with a rectangular head and a hooked nose reached out to shake my hand.

Mr. Keating was an investor. Years later he would become the biggest savings and loans bust in American history. That bastard cost the United States Government $3 billion before it was all said and done. His savings and loans company was insolvent for years but kept buying junk bonds hoping to turn it around. At the depths of his debt he had a net worth of negative $100 million. He went to prison.

That night, though, we were thick as thieves. Men like that have money in everything, and if they have any style, they buy cattle. He saw my talent as a breeder and he liked to drink. Bull 4-6003 made such and impression on him that he began paying me $25,000 a year to advise him on his cattle. This is while I was still at Superior Oil. He'd fly me out to Phoenix, first-class, put me up in a first-class hotel and I'd tell him how to breed his herd. We're talking $25,000 for a week's worth of work. His Santa Gertrudis were looking good, like really good. One day he sent me a check for $300,000. He said "Half is mine, half is yours. Go out and buy cows." Well, I bought them beeves and kept them for four or five years on his land, then sold them off and made $400,000.

The year 1979 was a gainful one for me and The Superior Land and Cattle Co. It started off in January where Bull 7-265 won Grand Champion at the Fort Worth Stock Show. In

February, the same bull took Reserve Grand Champion at San Antonio and Reserve Champion at the National Santa Gertrudis Show in Baton Rouge. In March, he took Grand Champion at the Rio Grande Valley Show, and another bull of ours won Reserve Grand Champion at Victoria. We were showing off. In April, I took a vacation. In May, we sold that second bull for $40,000, and we're talking 1979-dollars. It was the highest auction price paid for any Santa Gertrudis bull at the Western Heritage Sale in Houston. We partied that night. In June, another one of my bulls, 1-1500, sold for one hundred, one hundred dollar bills. The most paid at the Tri-Star Sale that year. In July, our two highest weaning-weight bull calves, had adjusted 205-day weights of 858 and 910 pounds. Some heavy mother fuckers. In August, we took that first bull, 7-265, to the Indiana, Ohio, and Kentucky State Fairs where he won Reserve Grand Champion at all of them. All of this traveling had me away from Di. In Indiana, I screwed a freckled redhead selling pies in a blue checkered summer dress behind the grandstand.

    She said, "Make me squeal, pig man." But, the microphone was still on and all of Indianapolis heard me correct her.

    "Cattle. Not pigs."

    In Ohio, it was the uptight event manager in her trailer, and in Kentucky, it was the wife of the auctioneer, who said I had a faster tongue than her husband.

    In September, my stud 7-265, won Grand Champion at the Washington County State Fair and the East Texas State Fair. In October, we won so many Grand Champions and Reserve Grand Champions across the South that it would waste my time listing them. In November, we sold several outstanding animals in Paraguay and Brazil including a bull for $25,000.

    And I know what you're going to say. I should have stayed faithful to Di. And you're wrong. It's true, all men need women, but not all need love. Some need a thing that's akin to love, it looks and smells like love, but it's something much less honest.

Man needs sex. Even if we are satisfied with the sex we're having with a gal, a healthy body will ramp up and overcompensate, just in case another one comes around. Can't no woman wear me out. I've studied herd sires. I know.

The difference with people is, the horndog feeling leaves us with guilt because we're told we shouldn't be attracted to anyone but our wives. And, since we're weak creatures, we think those horndog feelings must be floating around somewhere in our woman, too. We mark them with blame and fill up with jealousy, even when there's little evidence. It puts you in the soup. But, like I said, I was doing fine.

CHAPTER 19 ...
Cane's Last Trick

...On the first night, she ran me over in her van. She ran over every detail of me with her eyes and fingers after she gave me the sit-down tour. This is how she cooks, this is what she reads, here are some half-finished paintings.

...On the second night, she fixed pancakes with cacao nibs and honey. My camping spatula dripped from her fingers as it hovered and poked. I followed the arc up her tattooed wrist with honey.

...On the third night, she lectured the wolves. She spoke about graphic art and the meatpacking industry and she held their paws and tugged their ears. With a cigarette gripped in my big toothy smile, I'd applaud her and roll my head back and moan softly, happily, distantly.

...On the fourth night, she beat me in Scrabble and the wind ripped through the car crash gaps of the van and lifted our elementary words into a phantasmagorical whirl above the table, above the orange candle glow.

...And, on the fifth night, cashews were involved.

...On the sixth night, we walked to the Store. It was on the sixth night that we finally walked to the Store.

...

In the kitchen, I pointed Lou out to her. An old regular at the Store, Lou had a long cartoonish face that would have been ugly if it were out from under a cowboy hat. Eyebrows drooped so hard down the sides of his forehead that they were almost vertical, and his red porous nose looked to be the size of a pear. In rural Texas, the men have harsh names that fling out of your mouth like darts and stick to the wall. Names like Zane, Slade, Blain, Victor, Rex, and they go to places like "town" and "Victor's daddy's house." Lou had a soft name, though, like a one-note whistle. He had lost $100 in a drunken footrace around lunchtime earlier that day. A fifty-yard dash. Lou made it thirty-five, and had been trying to win back his money by rolling dice in a shallow cardboard box with two cowboys and a plumber. Ickie's daughter and I teethed on our beer bottles and talked while we leaned against the sink watching them gamble from a distance.

"Nine's the number, boys. Nine's the number," Lou said.

Six.

"Nope. Gotta come up. Nine's the number. Here comes nine...four. No good. Still gotta come up. Come on niner. Niner niner niner. Niner vagine-r."

"Ten against him," a cowboy dropped a bill curved down the center, the way they get when they've been handled and traded all night, held in sweaty hands with a thumb pressing too tight. The plumber threw in his counter, a silent reply, without looking up from the dice dancing in Lou's calloused paw. In the box, the bills looked like little landlocked canoes after a flood, facing all different directions.

"Come on niner. Niner vagine-r. Come on niner..." he hollered with his foggy eyes locked on an empty corner of the box. They rolled. Seven.

"Fuck."

"Chingado," the plumber said. The cowboy picked up the bills and stacked them efficiently in his palm.

Brittany said she was used to getting strange looks from folks...her hair the way it was, and tattoos. Her head was shaved on the sides and a mess of blonde dreadlocks fell down her back. A warrior of art, I think is the look she was going for. White people with dreadlocks are funny in their fascination with themselves. They're *daring* and *cultured*, at least until they tire of that particular brand of *daring* and *cultured* and start wearing kimonos. The white hairs on her shins looked like a child's when the light caught them crossways. The hairs on her legs reminded me of my sister's when she young, before she learned that her body and its humanness was a burden. We talked until Brittany had to piss and I stood around waiting for something to happen.

"You trying to clip me for a two-dollar beer, Lou?" Jennifer said behind the bar. She snatched across the bar top for the bottle in front of him. He must have reached over the counter when she wasn't looking to steal it, but was too naturally dumb to hide it and too naturally drunk to grab it up before she lunged. He just sat there on the stool open-mouthed with his shoulders hunched and his arms dangling between his knees on the sixth night of Brittany's visit.

Now that I think about it, her stay went something like this:

...On the first night, we realized one another's spontaneity. Spontaneity is held in high regard among painters and travelers and trick-shot pool players. We congratulated one another on one another's commitment to spontaneity.

...On the second night, I told her that since I liked her so much, she was allowed to lie to me as long as she could convince me of the details. She told me she didn't need my permission to do that.

...On the third night, we talked about our parents. I could tell she was lying, then.

...On the fourth night, we swam naked in the river. I held her and the water wrapped around our feet like ever-changing socks. The minnows kissed the moonlight bouncing off of our white asses.

...On the fifth night, cashews were involved.

...On the sixth night, we walked to the Store.

...

During one of her lectures in the van, Brittany suggested I kept a journal of my travels because I don't want to forget things, small things especially, and that our memories shift like the plates of the crust of the world, some hiding under others, reordering their shape if that shape goes unstudied allowing change without notice until their silent wrestling has redesigned the landscape of our own personal history, of the story we tell. Because:

...On the first night, we realized one another's spontaneity. Spontaneity is held in high regard among painters and travelers and trick-shot pool players. We congratulated one another on one another's commitment to spontaneity.

...On the second night, we traded sips of homemade prickly pear vodka brewed by a widow who lived near Enchanted Rock.

...On the third night, naked, she backed down a coyote with my old hatchet. Cane hid behind her legs and I sat by the fire with a cigarette in my big toothy smile, applauding her, rolling my head back and moaning softly, happily, distantly.

...On the fourth night, she beat me in Scrabble and the wind ripped through the cracked van door and lifted our elementary words into a phantasmagorical whirl above the table, above the orange candle glow.

...On the fifth night, cashews were involved.

...On the sixth night, we walked to the Store.

...

"That yo' van down acrosst the rivuh?" the old drunk asked me on the porch of the Store somewhere pushing midnight.

"Yes, sir."

"This'n yo' mutt?" he asked. Cane raised an eyebrow at the insult, even though he was a mixed-breed mongrel.

"Yes, sir," I said again.

"I had a dog like him once. Black, with stout haunches like that. Loved him more than air," he said.

"He's a good one," I said half at him, half at the stars.

"Y'knowwuh? I'll give you seventy dolla' for that mutt."

"He's not for sale, Lou. Why don't you get on?" I said.

"No. No. Eighty-five. Eighty-five because he look so much like my dead dog. See, I need a new friend."

Soggy black tobacco leaves spilled from of the butt end of my cigarette. It looked like a ponytail between my fingers. I kissed it to my mouth, then drew it away.

"You funny, Lou?" I asked.

"How you mean?" His chin rose and his milky alcoholic eyes slid over to meet mine for the first time, really.

"Do you know any jokes? I mean, can you tell 'em in a way that makes folks laugh?"

"Guessin' if it was the right crowd of folks, I could."

"Well, Cane likes a joke. You make him laugh, and you can have him." The old drunk came back at me with some confusion and I reassured him. I've seen the dog laugh, but only if something good happens. I asked Brittany to demonstrate.

My peachy assistant had been leaning with her back against a post on the porch. "Come here, lover. I'll tell you a joke," she said. Cane unwound himself on the concrete and walked over to her. She walked the dog down the steps and opened a tail gate to one of the trucks sitting in front of the building. Cane jumped in so he was eye level with the girl. Brittany grabbed his jowls in her palms, studying all sides of his head like it was a cube. A crowd of smokers and well diggers started to take interest and walked closer to hear what was happening. Brittany took one step back and recited her joke.

"An Aggie was on a trip to the Northeast over summer break. One night he went out for a drink in the big city. He saw this beautiful young woman sitting at the end of the bar. Now, he could tell she liked his look based off the way she gazed at his cowboy hat and boots. She asked him where he went to school. He said, 'I'm an Aggie. And, where do you go to school, pretty girl?'

"She said, 'Yale.'

"He said, 'WHERE DO YOU GO TO SCHOOL, PRETTY GIRL?!'"

Cane rolled over onto his back and started kicking into the air. Upside down, his cheek flaps fell upward and it showed his smiling teeth. He twisted and rolled his head back and forth for a little while, panting and having a time. He popped back to his feet and shook the dust off from nose to tail. The drunk crowd cheered for him and the story teller.

Lou walked to the center of the mob, held the bed of the truck to steady himself and looked around at the small crowd, waiting for them to quiet down.

"Ok, mutt, listen up. I got one," he said... "Why don't the Mexicans never have themselves a team when the Olympics come to town? Well, because all of 'em that can run, and jump and swim made it to Texas by now." One cowboy somewhere in the crowd gave a laugh, but for the most part the group was silent. So was Cane.

I reached a hand out and put it on Lou's shoulder. "I forgot to mention, partner. Cane's momma was a Chihuahua."

"No, see that's bullshit. It's just a party trick. You taught the dog to roll when you yell *pretty girl*. It's just a command. That joke's tired anyway. Plus, what's a dog know about fucking Yale?"

"Brittany?" I said.

"He's right. It is an old one," pursing her lips sarcastically.

"See. Bullshit. Let's have one of these old timers tell a groaner and see what he does." He looked around the truck. "Here, Glenn, you tell this dog a joke, see if you can get it to laugh," he said.

"No, no, no," I said. "The deal was you get one joke. If Cane ain't a fan, there's nothing to be done. Your old racist ass joke just ain't very likable, Lou."

"See, I didn't know the mutt was a spic. That's...How am I supposed to know that?" he said. The plumber giggled from the back of the crowd. "This dog reminds me so much of my old mutt. You gotta let me have him. I'm gonna shoot my goddamn self, son. I have nothing in this whole goddamn world. I got no land and I got a broken pick-'em-up truck." His voice tripped and slowed down. "My dog ran off a month after muh old lady died. She was everythang. A fuckin' saint. Ask any of these old timers how I was when she was around. They'll tell you I was a good man, a pure man when she was alive. I loved her through anything and that dog couldn't stand being around my crying ass when the Lord took her, so he left me too." He dropped to his knees, and cried with his knuckles in the gravel. His words were bubbling slowly out of the sides of his mouth, now. "She couldn't cook. She wasn't pretty like Bowersox here, but I loved her through anything."

He looked straight up and set his wet eyes on the same starry sky that every crying Texan was using that night to remember lost lovers. "Every evening she made this soup. And no, it wasn't good. It was rotten. It was so rotten that I had to fight back from gagging. Before we fell asleep at night she'd roll over and give me the lovingest kiss, but that soup had dried in her mustache and I'd get to gagging again. I miss her so much I wake up in the middle of the night dreaming with that taste on my lips."

Brittany, me, and the whole gang of stand-byers stood by in shock and confusion over that broken man. The story of Lou's life hung in the dusty air like a long tragic fart. Then through the silence, a snort rumbled from the back of the truck. The dog was trying to hold back his laugh. Young Cane couldn't help himself. He dropped to his back rolling in the bed of the truck panting and wheezing so violently it seemed like his body was inflating and deflating entirely. He was busting up harder than I'd ever seen. He was kicking so hard he put marks in the metal truck bed. He was convulsing wildly and for a long time, too. He finally stiffened, and a wail came out of him that was almost human, the most divine and clear sound of joy and relief, and when it was over the dog lied still with his eyes closed and mouth cracked open in a grin. We all stepped closer to the truck. Lou was still on his knees turning gravel into concrete.

Cane lied warm and heavy and I knew what had happened. I took a jacket that was lying across a spare tire in the bed of the truck and wrapped him in it as snug and gentle as I could. His joints bent meekly when I moved them into place. A lone tear rolled down my cheek and I wanted to see my sister.

I gave Brittany the keys and she drove while I held the dog across my lap. And now, thinking back, I remember the sour smell of that hot American river at midnight as I laid young Cane down on its banks. But that's all that comes back. The sour smell. Not the nakedness of the stars, not Brittany's hand on my back, not the disgust I felt for the old drunk, or the grace I must have wished upon him either.

Ickie's daughter is long gone now, living for effect, selling her art and seldom sees her father. I still don't write things down because like a joke, it's impossible to tell your story the same way twice. Its details, its phrasing, its build, its turn. You have to start the thing fresh to tell it right. Only its consequence comes back to us in recollection. As I lowered Cane into the sandy hole, I knew where Randy hid his money. The answer was above my head and below my bended knees. Some people praise the rain and some praise the river, but neither is better than the last. Rain is just the river before it touches mud; clean and on the right side of grace. After a loss, you swim. In grief, the river.

CHAPTER 20 ...
A Distracted Mind

    I threw the last shovelful of sand on top of Cane and started digging for the money. Randy must have used some kind of marker, I thought as I stepped on the shovel. An old tree, a post, a boulder. The tool moved on its own and my mind turned on itself. I was reminded of something Randy had written. Somewhere in middle age his book undertook philosophy. As I dug, I thought back to the story.

CHAPTER 21 …
Sweetest 7-iron Under Pressure

Now, there is a rumor that I'm the only man to ever get kicked out of Horseshoe Bay Country Club because I got caught screwing too many married women. But that's not true. There was one guy worse than me, and he screwed the husbands too. It was a shame to lose that house, though. Our backyard butted right up to the ninth fairway.

There is a difference between motivation and a man's allotted daily dose of vitality. Motivation is a directive force, and ambition is a directed one. Our motivations bloom somewhere outside us. I've always thought of ambition as a punch to be thrown. Some men don't know where or when to throw their punch. They have talent, advantages, good health, well-connected aunts and uncles but still find themselves dizzy in the ring taking swings at the referee. Even the wildest madman gets my respect though because he's eventually comforted in exhaustion. But idle men, they don't enjoy success or failure. They have restless minds because their bodies crave movement and shake with unused energy.

I was golfing with a man from South Africa who was in the States looking to buy some cows from me. It only took me three holes to seal the deal.

He said, "I like your cattle and I want to buy some. Now, I can pay you in cash, but I'd rather pay you in diamonds." That mother fucker pulled out a big bag of diamonds on the fourth tee box of the Horseshoe Bay Country Club.

I said, "Okay." We took it down to a well-known jeweler and got it appraised later that day. We got those diamonds for thirty-cents on the dollar. We made a lot of money just off the damn diamonds.

On the ninth hole, the South African teed off and put his ball right down the middle. My tee shot put me in the rough left of the fairway and right under my bedroom window. I hurried up to my ball, but Di saw me. She had suspicioned that I was sleeping around and must have found some evidence of it while I'd been away. My wife yelled down on me from the second story window like Juliet from the balcony.

"You mother fucker! I thought you loved me. I'm leaving you, Randy! All you ever do is golf just like my daddy."

There was an extra set of Titleists in the bedroom closet. They were a gift from Mr. Keating. It was a nice gesture by him and the bag had my name embroidered on it in gold lettering, but they were cut the wrong length and I didn't like the feel of the putter grip. She took the clubs out of the closet and threw them at me over-handed one at a time leaving divots in the fairway. Some of them stuck straight up out of the grass. I put my arm up to shield my head. I felt like a rattlesnake under a truck tire.

"Can I hit the shot first?" I yelled between club throws. "We're holding up play." The whole neighborhood was out in their backyards watching.

She'd retreated back into the house to get more shit to throw at me. I approached the ball and took my time. You can't rush your routine. I drew the club head back and heard her wrestling with the blinds in the window. With my club above my head ready to unwind, I saw the shadow of a television next to me on the grass. I don't know how, but my hands found the slot and I struck the ball clean. The T.V. whizzed past my head and the cord wrapped around the shaft of my club and yanked it out of my hands. Glass and plastic shattered just next to my foot. My shot landed five feet from the pin, thank God. If I chunked that shot she would have won. She would have won the ultimate fight. There would be proof that she got to me. That's pressure.

"Throw down the bag, honey. I'll clean this up." I yelled up at her, then looked around at all the clubs in the grass. "I'm over the limit down here."

In those days, Di and I were able to make up, but it got harder to do. We needed to reset. A marriage is full of resets. A reset is like wiping your boots clean. You know they'll get muddy again one day, but for the time it's restorative. It's usually just apologizing, deeply apologizing. It doesn't even have to be out loud. A look can be an apology enough.

Doubt is a bastard and jealousy is the dirty cousin of doubt. That's the fuel behind a fight. That's what threatens you in a barroom, or on a ball field. A fight needs a desperation. A fight needs desperation the way a tornado needs cold dry air. The weak man hates himself for needing to fight, and hates himself for the stirring that happens inside himself. This stirring looks bad in front of women which is why I don't fight unless I know I can win.

CHAPTER 22 ...
Looking for an End

The rain started at sunrise and washed away the stickiness from my arms and neck. Trucks and trailers passed on the bridge but I didn't care. I was looking for the end. To the northwest, the rain found runnels and trenches carved in the hillocks and meadows of Mason and Menard Counties. Muddy water surged into its local creek and dumped into the Llano. Dense and unmoving, a tempest dropped rain on my shoulders and on that hard Texas earth. While I dug, the story of the money played in my head.

CHAPTER 23 ...
Tough Old Bird

We started a family in Horseshoe Bay but it was all ending. I knew the divorce was going to be rough because we had been vicious to one another. She'd started cheating on me and we were stuck in a game of cat and mouse trying to catch one another. The paranoia made me wild and I was away from home a lot. Around that time, I took the trip to Brownsville and had the stroke on the golf course. This is the period of my life that I have struggled for decades to recall but cannot. All I can do is speak in large generalities about where I was and what I was doing. I know that we still had the house in Horseshoe Bay, but I was spending a lot of time at the old ranch house in Castell. I know that I buried the money in Castell and not Horseshoe Bay because it is where I had the privacy and the land. Burying your own money is an old rancher tradition. I wouldn't have done it on a golf course. It's something you do at home. Castell has always been my home.

Shortly after the divorce I went back to the country for good. I bought an old house in town on the south side of the river, and got to work getting Castell recognized for what it is, a beautiful and cruel pocket of central Texas, beautiful for the flowers in the springtime that are so vivid that the pastures look like bowls of children's breakfast cereal, and cruel because of the heat and storms that can lie on top of this land and leave you helpless.

June, 1997, the Llano River rose to 39.91 feet. We almost reached the record which was set in 1935 at 41.5 feet. I was home in 1997 when Bandera, which is a few counties to the south, got eighteen inches of rain in two days. Tornadoes touched down all along the Llano Uplift.

There's an old lady that comes up to the Store named Maxine Bremburg. She's ninety-eight years old. Every Sunday she eats an entire ribeye to herself, and all the trimmings, and kisses me on the mouth before she leaves. She's what people call a tough old bird. Back in 1997, when those tornadoes were spinning across ranches all over the hill country, her and her husband walked over a hundred yards from their back porch through sheets of rain and wind into an antique barn that was on their property. It's an old stone barn, erected in the late 1800s by her husband's grandfather. They walked to the sturdy old barn, holding on to one another so they didn't get blowed over, and climbed into a ranch truck that he had parked inside. The old man behind the steering wheel, and Maxine holding his hand from the passenger seat, listened to the wind that was strong enough to rip the asphalt off of Highway 152. It picked fish up out of ponds and landed them miles away. My good friend Sam Walter, found a five-pound catfish on top of his truck just flopping there like a hood ornament. He kept it. Maxine and her husband sat in that pickup imagining the horror of what was happening outside. They heard the thud of chickens and newborn calves being blown against the stone wall of the old German barn. Still, the wall didn't cave in. When the tornado was right on top of them, the wooden roof peeled off overhead. The old couple looked at one another. He told her, they'd be alright. Those barns were meant to last. Just then, a two-by-four shot through the wooden barn door, through the windshield of the truck and straight through his chest like a needle through cotton. She sat there waiting the storm out, while her husband was tacked to the driver's seat of his pick-up. Afterwards, the whole town pitched in, helping her recover. Later that week, on a sunny day, a crew of men unwrap three hundred yards of barbed wire from her chimney.

That's the cruelty, and it makes the beauty shine more beautiful. But, there are a lot of beautiful places in Texas. City folks have a lot of options. If you want them to come to your spot you need a gimmick. You have to give them a reason to make the trip. I had the river, and the lawlessness (Two terms as County Commissioner gave me plenty of pull with the Sheriff. We don't see police around here.). We had great burgers, and at the beginning I basically gave the beer away for free. Everyone was a friend, but I still didn't have a gimmick.

On a trip to Las Cruces with my girlfriend, we stumbled into a little Mexican bar outside of the city in the foothills. The roof was peeling off and the floor was made of concrete and fixed with a layer of dirt, kind of like the General Store. There were chickens running around eating tortilla chip crumbs under the tables. A place has to have a feeling to it, and this little taberna had feeling. For some reason, I had my eye on the big red rooster that ruled the flock. He was a Rhode Island Red and for some reason I was drawn to it. He reminded me of the chickens we had on the farm when I was a child. I asked how much for the bird and the bartender told me that he was not for sale, then I saw her glance down at my girlfriend's wrist. She said that in exchange for the cock, she would take Karen's watch. I slipped it off her thin wrist, kissed her on the cheek and said I'd make it up to her. We brought that rooster back home and named it Cockaroo.

He fit right in. He was an absolute gentleman taking care of all the hens, and getting his poke with each of them every day. One morning, I was going through boxes of junk I had brought to Castell from my home in Horseshoe Bay. I wanted to throw it all away and just forget the divorce, but I had to be careful. It was over a year after the stroke and I still hadn't remembered I'd hid the cash and I was starting to get concerned I'd never find it. Cash would have been helpful in those times. I had quit The Superior Oil Company after the stroke and had started out on my own buying cattle and managing the herd in

Castell. It was possible there was a clue buried somewhere in one of the moving boxes. When I got frustrated, I started throwing things from the boxes. Clothes, decorations, dishes, tools. It was all spread out in the hot shed behind my new old house. Cockaroo strutted into the shed. I didn't pay him any attention. I was becoming delirious and a little heat stroked. Then, music started playing behind me. Spinning around, I saw the rooster humping the Billy Bass. In that moment, my gimmick was born! I swooped him up in one arm, picked the fish up in the other and ran to the Store. Cockaroo jumped out of my arms when we got into the bathroom.

"Stay here. We don't need you getting eaten by a coyote." He hoped on the edge of the toilet bowl. On my way out the front door of the Store, I set the toy fish on the shelf I had there and got to work building a pin for Cockaroo outside next to the shed. I drove the t-posts into the hard soil with a smile on my face, shaking my head. I went back to the bathroom, and when I opened the door the rooster was pissing in the toilet and had a cigarette in its beak. He must have picked it up off the bathroom floor but couldn't find a match. I tucked him up under my arm like a football and walked over to the pin and set him down gently. I plucked the cigarette out of his mouth and tossed it in the grass.

"We need to keep you alive," I said. When the first folks showed up that evening, I was nervous. It was a couple of locals, regulars and friends. I bought them rounds of beer and mixed some hooch for the ones I knew would take it. I was making sure they were in good spirits for the show. "Follow me," I said, and grabbed the fish off the shelf and walked outside and around to the side of the building.

Under the shade, the crowd huddled around the rooster's pin and smoked and spit and mumbled to one another.

"They's usually two cocks in a cockfight, Randy," one of the smartass well diggers said to me and took a swig of his beer. Cockaroo sashayed around the perimeter, eyeing the audience.

"Whip it out, then," I said to him while I was clearing all the straw and bottle caps from the area so my performer didn't get distracted. I set the Billy Bass down in the dirt outside of the pin and Cockaroo's strut slowed and he pressed his beak through the chicken wire. I pulled open the little gate and he ambushed the little toy. He stomped the red button and the robot started flopping. The rooster hoped on and lowered his wings around the rubber fish.

"Go, Cockaroo! Go! Go! Go!" I spread my feet and bent over the bird and pumped my fists. He finished in less than five seconds and stood over it looking around at the crowd. "Anybody got a cigarette?" I said.

Cockaroo caught on and word got out about the rooster. People would come up all the way from Austin and San Antone. I couldn't keep up with the crowds. We sold out of beer and burgers every weekend that summer. Some housewife put a video of Cockaroo on the internet. You can look it up. I had to buy more kayaks and feed. They was so many people coming out here, I actually went in to the county offices and got my liquor license and all the permits to sell food. We was on the map. It looked like the Pinta Trail out here, people would roll in thirsty and leave sunburnt and happy. Shit, the news even came out and did a little story on Cockaroo and the Store. One Saturday, he performed twenty-seven times, plus all of the pokes he had with all of the hens. Folks would come out to see the Store and love it so much they decided they had to stay. Before it was all over, I had made $253,000 in commission on real estate deals.

CHAPTER 24 …
A New Liquid Order

The wooden handle of the shovel was engorged with rain water, and clumsy, but it was the only warm thing that touched me. Pink blood filtered through my wrinkled white fingers and down the handle toward the hole. The blade slid in and out of the liquefied earth under darkened skies and my soaked boots. Heavy droplets hit my eyelids and tried to close them. My shirt was thirty yards behind me fixed to the riverbank, held down with permanent sand. The lapping water dumped into the silver holes along the river's edge. Some people praise the rain, and some praise the river, but neither is better than the last. Rain is just the river before it touches mud; clean and on the right side of grace.

Young trees hung canted above me, their heads tilted in a uniformed mutilation, all confused by me and by the source of their pain. Nothing was in the mud besides my shovel. I worked my way from the bridge up the swollen and jungly river, parallel to Randy's ranch house. Starting a new hole, I pressed the tip of the spade into the soft loam and jumped on it. It sank half a foot and stopped. When the shovel hit, it didn't crunch or thud, but bounced off something hollow. Not a rock. I looked back toward the bridge with my mouth open, still balancing on the step of the shovel. Brown logs piled against the edge of the bridge and the water sucked through the cluster into the hollows below. The wind blew against my chest and I took a slow step backwards. I hadn't realized it, but I had been working my way up the sloped bank, avoiding the rising water. The line of holes behind me led down into the river. When I'd started those holes, they'd been on dry ground. In the thin morning light, the river was a caramel-colored kingdom moving past me to its own decree, and it pushed the debris forward and upward as it surged. The muddy lot that held the van and my campsite was hidden under two feet of foaming water. Vine-tied logs were wedged around the tires and pinned beneath the undercarriage, pressing and threatening. Barn wood and other dreck was held tight against the rear bumper with fast folding water. The slanted trees along the opposite bank had been swallowed, the top boughs waved brave green leaves just above the surface suggesting a surrender.

My shovel still rested in the silt atop the buried container. The water came toward me, up the bank, and hugged the blade of the shovel. I pulled it out of the ground and the edges of the gash were softened by the receding stream. I threw the shovel back into the earth and felt the same bounce, I pulled it out and shoved it deep down a foot to the right of the buried package.

I ran up the river's edge, waded out to the van and tried to push the floating debris out toward the middle of the river. I broke some small branches loose, and they peeled out, rushing downstream, but leg-sized logs and panels of barn wood held solid against the back of the tires. Loose branches floating in the water had knotted into one another, creating floating islands of heavy dross that rolled down the river like cannon balls. One rammed through the back of my legs and lodged under the bumper rocking the van forward.

The door roared open and I climbed in. I grabbed the rag off the bench and wiped the water from my face. It smelled like motor oil, and left black smudges down my cheeks. I looked like a crying clown in black and white. Water rolled through the open door and settled around my feet. In the driver's seat, I pushed my cold black hair back and slid the dry baseball cap over my head. Rattling and steaming, the engine started anxiously. I let off the brake and felt for the river behind me. Still heavy on the ground, I cut the wheel to the left and aimed uphill. I gave it more gas and the tires slid. The rear end swung around, pushed by the water, but it wouldn't climb. Perpendicular to the ranch house, and half-sunk, I looked up the hill and hit the accelerator. The tires felt for the rocky granite bottom and the van started to bounce as they spun over the stones. I started to ascend the hill slowly.

I saw it coming from my left, distorted through the rain glass window, a live oak, black and shiny in the grey morning, roots-first. The van rocked and spun upstream, floating backwards. Tools crashed in the back and the frame of the van creaked from the unfamiliar twisting. My kitchen floated up into the cab. A couple bananas, the dog bowl, the dish soap. The engine cut out. I stood up in the moving van, and my life orbited me. Things floated by, spinning in the water, shuffling themselves into a new liquid order. With one hand above my head holding the ceiling, I shuffled through the loud knee-high water to the back of the van and opened a drawer. The red poker chip rattled and rolled across the spoons and forks. I picked it up and the bands around the outside began to spin. My hand was pale and furrowed from the water. Blood from my blister fell down my wrist. I tucked it into the band of my cap before I bailed out the side door.

Slanted in the water upstream, the shovel held its place. As I ran toward it, I heard the van slam into the concrete bridge.

I pressed the toe of my boot against the back of the shovel blade underwater then drew it out of the ground. I planted the other foot downstream to brace against the current. With each draw of the shovel, the water pushed me back and spun me off my mark. I felt for the hole with my foot and thrusted the shovel down and felt the hollow bounce. I dove under, holding the anchored shovel. The water pressed my eyeballs deeper into my head. I could see my arms, pale white and blurry in the mud-brown water, one out extended, holding the shovel, and the other digging through the mud. The red cylinder shone in the water as I pulled away fistfuls of earth. I came back up for a breath, re-tightened the shovel into the ground and dove back down. The lip of the can was just broad enough to wrap my fingers around. I let go of the shovel, put both hands on the half-buried coffee can and let the current pull my body. I was completely extended when a log rammed into my neck and broke me loose from the ground. I tucked the can against my stomach. The skin on my neck and shoulder throbbed hot, bleeding in the sunless river. Curled into myself, I was an embryo again, undead, tumbling backwards. I found air and gasped it in. A glow came from the yellow van as I floated past it under water. I kicked and lined my body up with the hollow under the bridge. I swept through it and out the other side. I bobbed up out of the water and looked around. With the can tucked in one arm and my nose barely out of the water, I saw my way out. A powerline was dangling just above the surface about fifty yards downstream. I bent my arm at the elbow and raised it out of the water. A quick hot jolt would shoot through me and complete the circuit. As I moved toward the wire I tucked my chin into my shoulder and gritted my teeth waiting for the shock to end this trip. I squeezed my eyes shut, hoping they would stay in my head when the electricity passed through me and into the ionized water. That way my sister and dad could identify my body if they recovered it. My toes curled in my boots as my arm hooked around the cold black rubber wire. I bobbed there a second. A fucking whole second. A lifetime.

    My lower half was still being tugged downstream and it was a long way to the bank. I palmed the coffee can in one hand and wrapped that elbow around the lifeline. I pulled my feet out of the water and wrapped my ankles above the cable as well. I started pulling myself toward the Store on the south side of the river. It was slow progress pulling with one hand and incrementally inching my other arm up the line. When I reached the utility pole, I was still above water. Resting on the top rung, I shook my arms to regain feeling and strength. I tilted my head back and opened my mouth to the rain. The bank was only twenty or so yards away, so I threw the coffee can onto dry land. It would be easier to swim the twenty yards to shore with two arms instead of one. I climbed down the pole slowly, lowered my body into the brown eddy and started swimming. The muscles in my legs and shoulders shuttered and locked as I swam, but I made it to shore and crawled up the mud. I sat like a dog on all fours and hung my head panting in the sand.

"Whatchu got here, Doodah?"

I looked up at Jennifer examining the Folgers can. Behind her, the side-by-side sat idling, a deer rifle in the passenger seat.

"You should have just shot me on the wire," I said hanging my head again, my ribs expanding as they took in air. "It would have been a lot cleaner."

"Shoot you? Why'd I do that for?" she said, and tossed the can down the hill. It rolled and stopped under my nose. I flopped to my side and dropped my hip in the sand. Wet and frayed, the duct tape peeled off easily, and the plastic lid slurped and popped. Inside, wrapped in a thin sheet of clear plastic tarp, a little blue book, worn and damp. The Adventures of Huckleberry Finn. I stared at the cover, turned it over and back again and looked up at Jennifer. I started to smile.

"Where's the money?" I asked. She wasn't laughing. In fact, she was serious, almost sorry looking.

"There ain't no money," she said wincing in the rain.

"You read Randy's book," I said. "He buried money all over Castell. You've been looking for it."

"Yeah, I read it. But I don't gotta dig one hole to know there ain't no money."

"How do you know? It's in his book. The money, the stroke."

"I know what the book says," she said. "I wrote it."

"What?" I scrambled slowly to my feet. "No. It was his life."

"It was his life. Now it's fiction, honey."

"You can't lie about a man's life," I said.

"Faking someone's life is as easy as faking your own. If you knew Randy, you knew everything he said was fiction, mixed in with a little vodka and a lot of showmanship." The rain hit her mascaraed eyelashes. "I worked for the man for a decade. I knew him better than anyone. Come on, let's dry you out."

I climbed into the buggy next to her without speaking, Randy's entire story replaying in my head. The cap gun and the snake, the Mexican assassins, the wife.

"You made up the wife? You made it all up?"

"No, Doodah. Not all of it," she said.

I put my hand on the top of my head. My hat was gone. The poker chip was gone. We drove up the hill to the Store.

"I didn't bury that book, though," she said glancing down at my lap where the cartoon Huck smiled up at me. "That one is between you and Randy."

"But what about the prescription pad from the nurse girlfriend? She was in the memoir."

"You found a prescription pad? God, he always denied that one. Even to me," she said.

"Why did you do this? I almost died chasing sand."

"I needed a gimmick." I sat in the passenger seat and grew goose bumps from being cold and wet.

"I was a test run." I said to myself, but she heard me over the pattering of the small engine.

"That book is my fuckin' rooster. My Cockaroo. People will come to look for this money and I'll be here to sell 'em burgers and ball caps. A modern-day treasure hunt. We'll be in the news. Randy will live on. Castell will live on." I sat back in the seat and looked straight ahead. "And, I told you to stay on the south side. It floods down there. I told you that."

"What's the gun for?" I asked.

"When the power goes out, the meth-heads get a little braver," she said.

"The Store doesn't have power?"

"No, not since late last night."

"I thought it was my big rubber boots that kept me from getting shocked," I said.

"That's not how it works," she said. "Not even close."

When we pulled up to the Store, Ickie was standing on the porch smoking a cigarette. "I thought you weren't gonna make it, dude. I's like shit, he's a goner. He's goosed. Nuthin' I could do, y'know."

"I know," I said, walking past him through the doors.

CHAPTER 25 …

Bulldacious

"But you hanged on, man. You b'long in the circus," he said, with a beer in his hand. I was walking with purpose to the back room, but he kept following me. "I remember one time, a few years back, ev'body had these flyers on they windshields…Circus in town, Circus, in town, all over ev'body's cars. Here's a buys-one-gets-one free pass type deal, so I went to it, y'know. Turns out it's a circus and rodeo."

I climbed the loft while Ickie leaned against the ladder and kept talking. "So, at the circus they had trapeze and all that, and they got this big, uh, cage…ball, like a globe. And the motorcycles go inside and ride around and shit, upside down, and they come out. And they did all that shit. Ok, so the circus is over, now the rodeo starts. It's the same guys that was on the motorcycles that are riding the freakin' bulls. They were doing the trapeze and all that shit. Same people. Just changed outfits. That's what you should do, man. I saw you on that wire trapeezing. Just got that in your blood. We could make money doin' that. You ever ride a bull?"

Up in the loft, the pages were gone, the typewriter was gone. Jennifer had taken it. I walked back out to the bar with Ickie trailing me.

"Y'know, like the bull, Bulldacious, that mother fucker, nobody could ride him for like three hunerd rides. Nobody could ride him. He was a nasty mother fucker. So then, I bet you could ride it." He poked his stiff finger toward me with the rest of his hand still wrapped around the beer and his eyes fixed wide to the back of my head. "If you ride that bull…and you got people gamblin' in Vegas, they'll bet against you, but then you ride the mother fucker, y'know. So, you bank in."

"Where's the book?" I asked Jennifer who was behind the bar chewing on a soft wet piece of beef jerky.

"If you want a copy of the book, you'll be able to buy one this July. It'll have a cover and everything."

"We were friends, Jennifer. I almost died out there."

"I didn't intend for you to drown yourself. I was just seeing if you'd stick around a while. And you did. I told you I don't need friends. You know how many men come in here and want to be my friend?"

"You knew I was desperate. You wanted me dead. A kid dying in the pursuit of Randy's money would have just added to your story," I said. She picked a piece of jerky out of her teeth with her pinky nail and raised her eyebrows.

"Fuck this. I'm out of here." Soggy and brown, my wallet smelled musty when I pulled it out of my pocket. "I want a kayak," I said and placed three wet twenty-dollar bills on the counter. "And some beef jerky." As she turned around to grab the bag off of the shelf behind her, I reached down and slid the pack out of her back pocket.

"I'll throw in a life jacket for another five," she yelled across the empty grey barroom opening the fresh pouch of jerky and grinning.

"It'll fuck up my tan," I said, as I walked out the double doors. The rain had turned to a light sprinkle and droplets light as air clung to the hairs on my chest like thousands of apples balancing on thousands of sword blades. I opened the bag of body-warm jerky and dumped the remaining pieces into my mouth. Walking quickly, I snatched the little blue book out of the side-by-side and sealed it shut inside the empty jerky pouch. Ickie ran out the door after me.

"I would take yuh tuh town but all the creek crossin's gon be like frickin' over my Jeep, y'know."

"I know. Thanks, man."

"Here, dude. Gonna get cold," he said, unbuttoning his grease stained field coat, and handing it to me. I pulled the warm dry fabric over my arms and tucked the little blue book in the breast pocket. "Hey, man, you get to Austin, find the A-A-A Auto Body of Austin shop," He said it just like that, not triple-A, but , A-A-A. "Tell them Icarus Greene sent you an' they'll put you up in the back. They got a cot back there for travelers and bums and all kinds o' people like you that need stayin' for a night."

"Thanks, Ickie," I said. He put is cigarette in his mouth, then held his clenched hand in the air between us. I reached up, and for the first time in my life, bumped fists and meant it.

I walked across the street to the kayak barn and found my vessel, army green with no holes. I threw it over my shoulder and grabbed a paddle.

Goddamn, the water was fast, and not always below me. The deep channel was going the right way, and it was taking anyone with it. Trees, kayaks, vans, dog-faced white boys from the Midwest. I wanted out immediately, but the current was jealous and tugged me forward like I was on tracks, so I stayed in and urinated in my plastic seat. Reverse stroking around boulders, logs, sheds, drowning cattle, I swallowed the river, wiped it from my eyes and wanted to live. No screams, just reactions and corrections and quivering muscles. After an hour or so, I aimed for the river's edge and spun out clipping a log, then wobbled, unafraid of tipping. I reached land.

On the bank, I estimated another few hours to Llano at the pace I was moving. I watched the hill country float by in bits of debris. Huck Finn in a flat brimmed hat, waved to me as he drifted by with a smile. Bull 4-6003 stood red and proud on the deck of his raft, Jim held the halter of the beast. The clouds peeled back and let the sun drop its palm on my head and warm my wet hair. I closed the book and put it back in my pocket.

The rest of the river was wider and flatter with less rocks and fewer threats. All things dangerous moved by slower and wearier as if they had lost interest in me. The bridge over the Llano drew closer. Approaching the town, I pulled out of the river and into someone's unfenced backyard where a panicked little brown dog barked at the half-submerged doghouse he was tied to. I drug the kayak up into the yard and looked into the back window of the house. There was no one inside. I walked past the dog and waded out into the water and felt for the stake that held the end of his rope. I untied it underwater and approached the little mutt, holding steady to his rope. I took the collar off his neck. He smelled my hand and was thankful. I tied one end of the rope to an overhead tree branch, and the other end to the bow of the kayak that sat in the glossy wet grass. As I lowered the dog into the seat of the boat, he sniffed at the bag in my breast pocket.

I knew the bridge over the Llano supported the main north-south road through town. I walked the street with my thumb out, not expecting any play. My clean boots made me look respectable and, and it must have been my wet jacket that made the old man sympathetic to my condition. Tires crunched wet gravel behind me.

"Where you going, son?"

"It'll be summer soon. I thought I'd make my way north." He looked up the road. We were barely out of town.

"You can ride with me to Dallas, but I'll have to let you out there."

"That'll work," I said, and climbed in through the passenger door. Before he pulled back onto the highway, I saw him look into his rearview mirror as if he were puzzled.

"That yours?" he asked. I turned around and saw the little brown dog trotting after the truck.

"I guess it is," I said, and opened the door. The frail little thing hopped up into my lap and panted with his tongue hanging out of his mouth.

"Well, how far north you going?" he asked. I could tell he was the type of man who often gave in to his own unruly curiosity.

"St. Louis," I said. "Home."

Made in the USA
Lexington, KY
13 September 2019